PRAISE FOR CB SAMET

Four-time award winning author

GRAY HORIZON: 2019 Readers' Favorite Bronze Winner in Thriller category

MASTERS FILE: 2018 Readers' Favorite Honorable Mention in Romantic Suspense category

"… a fast-paced tale of crime and unexpected humor.… a combination of romance and suspense that lures the reader in, making it a one-sitting read."

— READERS' FAVORITE REVIEWER ON MASTERS FILE

"CB Samet is a master of the craft."

— READERS' FAVORITE REVIEWER ON WHYTE KNIGHT

SULLIVAN FILE

THE RIDER FILES BOOK 6

CB SAMET

For Vivienne

A phenomenal physician and friend
who gave more than a little inspiration for Jessica's character

1

---

*L*ori Sullivan exited the elevator and walked briskly through the dim parking deck. She tightened her wool coat more snugly to protect her against the biting Chicago chill as she neared her car.

The hospital should invest in better lighting for the deck, she thought. Half of the bulbs were burned out.

A faint scuffling of rubber soles on the concrete flooring pricked her ears. Was it another person, or had she mistaken the sound? The noise could have been a discarded paper cup scraping the concrete as the wind pushed it across the ground.

She walked faster, glancing at a security camera as she passed. Too bad they didn't offer any actual security. She'd heard a colleague had once asked for the footage to be reviewed after her car's bumper had been swiped, only to be told the parking deck cameras had been disabled due to budget cuts. They were nothing more than plastic perches for the pigeons.

Lori reached her car and locked her doors as soon as she was inside the vehicle. Thankfully, she'd thought to remote start her

Acura, so the engine and cab were already warm. In haste, she left the parking garage and drove toward home.

In the safety of her vehicle, she wondered if she'd only imagined being followed in the garage. Perhaps someone had been walking to work rather than toward her, although the late hour was after the night shift change.

She strummed her fingers impatiently on the steering wheel. Her nerves had been on edge all week.

Why hadn't Jess called yet? Since Lori worried her phone might be bugged, she didn't want to call Jess first and alert her pursuers about the USB Lori had created. She didn't want to make Jess a target. But maybe, despite her careful efforts, she already had.

She needed her friend's help. Jessica Ong would have the tenacity and resources to expose illegal activity. She knew people in the security business, and her brother was an investigative reporter.

On the interstate, Lori began driving erratically, watching the headlights behind her.

There.

She sucked in a deep breath as one driver repeatedly changed lanes in order to follow her. An icy fist closed over her chest. She couldn't go home.

Certain she was being followed, she sped up and considered how to lose the tail. She needed somewhere to hide until she could assimilate the information she'd collected into a cohesive presentation for the authorities. Home no longer felt safe now that she had confirmation someone was after her.

Danger was exponentially escalating. What she'd thought of initially as a conspiracy theory she'd concocted had proven terrifyingly true.

She needed to speak with Jess. As she reached for her phone, the vehicle behind her closed the distance.

*C*ALL *me as soon as you can.*

Jess stared at the text message from her work colleague, Lori Sullivan.

Before Jess could call her back, Austin poked his head into the physicians' workroom. "Dr. Ong, bed four's sats are dropping."

Jess pocketed her phone, pushed the chair away from the desk, and stood. Dropping oxygen saturations required a direct assessment for possible intervention. "Let's have a look," she told the nurse. She would call Lori back after she handled the current patient crisis.

She exited the physicians' workroom and followed Austin down the hall to bed four, her comfy clogs silent on the linoleum floor. Accustomed to the beeps of various machines—vital signs monitors, ventilators, renal replacement therapy—audible even in the hallways, Jess tuned them out.

Through the glass partition, she saw her patient. Mrs. Monroe was a young suburban soccer mom—probably with 2.5 kids and a minivan. She was much too young to be in Jess's ICU with respiratory failure. Despite the high-flow nasal canal device she wore, Mrs. Monroe still sucked air as if she'd just finished a soccer sprint down the full three-hundred-and-sixty-foot playing field.

"She's tiring," Jess told the nurse beside her, craning her neck to look up at him.

Austin, a big, burly nurse with a disproportionately quiet voice, asked, "You want to intubate her?"

"Yes," she agreed reluctantly, hating that the patient's condition had progressively worsened. "We've exhausted supportive measures. We'll intubate before she completely tuckers out."

"I'll let the respiratory therapist know. You want your usual cocktail for intubation?" he asked.

"Yes, thanks. I'll put in orders for fentanyl, sedatives, and paralytics. With the severity of her ARDS, she might need to be paralyzed for twenty-four hours to adequately oxygenate her."

Jess entered the room and plucked the stethoscope off a hook near the vital signs monitor and then listened to Mrs. Monroe's breath sounds. They were coarse, as if Velcro filled her chest rather than delicate organic lung tissue.

As she explained to the patient how she planned to put a breathing tube in and put her on mechanical ventilation, Jess's mind churned with the details of this case and the insufficient medical explanation for the woman's respiratory failure. She was suffering from adult respiratory distress syndrome—or ARDS—but the cause of her condition eluded Jess.

Within a few minutes, the respiratory therapist rolled the ventilator in the room, and Austin entered with a pocketful of the drugs Jess usually employed for sedation.

With proper personal protective equipment donned, Jess ran through the pre-procedure checklist with the team. She made a mental note to call the patient's husband after the intubation and let him know the turn of events.

"Short Asian coming through," Jess announced as she finagled her way through wires and IV tubing to the head of the bed. "Lower the bed, please."

Time to insert the tube and save a life. Hopefully.

The patient needed mechanical ventilation but providing life support didn't automatically mean she would recover from her mysterious illness. Sometimes life support bought the body time to heal, sometimes it only delayed the inevitable. In Mrs. Monroe's case, only time would tell.

WHEN JESS'S shift ended at seven a.m., she sat in the physicians' work room giving sign-outs on each patient to her friend and colleague, Jenna Masters. The room was a windowless square with six computers in cubicles along the walls. The single door was closed to keep out the boisterous noise of the ICU.

Jess had saved the update on Mrs. Monroe for last. "I had to tube her last night and paralyze her. If she gets worse, the next steps are prone or even ECMO."

"She's so young," Jenna marveled. Her long, copper hair was pulled back in a messy bun, and she wore scrubs like Jess.

"And we don't have an etiology yet. Infectious diseases are all ruled out. She didn't have any exposures to suggest hypersensitivity pneumonitis. She's not taking any prescription drugs that could cause acute lung disease. Her tox screen was positive for narcotics, but her husband said she had an oxycodone prescription six months ago for a torn rotator cuff, so maybe she popped a few of those recently and that's where the narcs came from. CT imaging shows classic acute lung injury with bilateral infiltrates. Can you lavage her lungs and check for eosinophils?"

"You're thinking eosinophilic pneumonia?"

"The pattern doesn't fit, but we need to keep ruling out everything we can think of."

"I'll take care of it," Jenna said.

"You might have to pull the trigger on giving her steroids." Steroids were the drug doctors loved to hate. They saved lives, but at a high cost with brutal side effects—muscle wasting, poor wound healing, hyperglycemia, weight gain, and the list went on.

Jess rubbed at her temples as her tired eyes watered, reminding her how long and busy her twelve-hour shift had been. "I had a case just like this last month in Chicago."

"You're still doing shifts up there? When are you going to settle here in Atlanta?"

Jess straightened and gave Jenna a pointed look. "When I have a reason to."

"Reece?" Jenna cringed.

Jess had met Reece at Jenna's wedding a few years ago. Since then, Reece and Jess had an on-again off-again roller-coaster relationship, which was currently off.

"The man does not have his shit together," Jess complained. "Anyway, my case in Chicago was an eighteen-year-old who took some new street drug—Luminous. His condition was also a mystery ARDS, until we learned about the drug from his girlfriend."

"Luminous? Never heard of it. What's in it?"

"No idea. Maybe narcotics. Maybe it's a designer drug. His urine drug screen was pan positive because he'd taken other drugs with it. Dr. Lori Sullivan and I had six Luminous patients we wrote a case series article about. It wasn't accepted for publication though. We're trying a different journal. Damn. I was supposed to call Lori back." She bit her lip at the sudden remembrance.

She had gotten tied up with emergencies through the night, and by two a.m. when things had slowed down, she figured it was too late to call Lori. The only important topic between them was research, and it could wait.

"Did the patients in your case series survive?" Jenna asked.

"Only half."

"You don't think soccer mom here took the designer drug?"

"I haven't heard of this street drug surfacing in Atlanta."

"Quite the mystery," Jenna said, brushing a rogue strand of

hair out of her face. "What about that case Arti had a few weeks ago? That was unidentified ALI."

"That acute lung injury turned out to be a patient on an experimental study drug. Arti submitted it to the pharmaceutical company as a possible adverse event related to the drug. And I asked Mrs. Monroe's husband—she's not enrolled in any treatment trials. So, her illness remains a mystery."

REECE OWEN ROLLED and sprang to his feet as he managed a well-placed right hook. The man he'd clocked stumbled backward. While the man rocked off-balance, Reece looped the toe of his boot around the man's ankle and tripped him. The two-hundred-and-fifty-pound Hispanic crashed to the ground.

Seizing the opportunity to gain the advantage, Reece pounced. He rolled the man over and secured his hands behind his back with a twist tie.

"I believe that's a new record." He stood and dusted off his jeans, more for effect than actual dirt. In fact, he hadn't even broken a sweat taking down his opponent.

"This isn't a hog-tying competition." His partner, Santino Alonso, wrestled on the floor with another man.

"No?" Reece cocked his head to one side, watching the rookie struggle to gain the upper hand against a nasty opponent. "Kinda looks like it is."

Santino's sienna skin glowed red from exertion. "*Hijo de mil puta!*" he yelled at the man he fought with before elbowing him in the ribs.

With a forced exhalation of pain, the man loosened his grip long enough for Santino to flip him and pin him facedown with a knee in his back.

Reece arched an eyebrow. "You kiss your sister with that mouth?"

Santino tied the man's wrists together behind his back with a plastic twist tie. "I don't have a sister. And you're one to talk." He stood up, catching his breath as he wiped blood off his lip with the back of his hand.

"I am reforming," Reece countered. "I've averaged only two quarters in my swear jar per week."

"Oh, yeah? I read somewhere that swearing can be a sign of intelligence."

One of the restrained men was cursing loudly at Reece and Santino, foam and spittle spewing as if he was a rabid dog. The two kidnappers lay on the floor of a dilapidated one-story house Reece and Santino had infiltrated. Because of the struggle, rickety furniture had been displaced in the living room and the battered coffee table and lamp had been knocked over.

"Can you verify that claim was substantiated with solid scientific evidence?" Reece stroked his mustache. "These men do not possess an abundance of wit or wisdom."

Santino shrugged.

Another Rider team member entered the room, gun drawn.

"Pleasant of you to grace us with your presence," Reece said. "As you can see, the rookie and I have handled the situation."

Ryan Walsh, Reece's long-standing partner, holstered his weapon. His broad shoulders filled the entrance. "And the girl?"

Reece jerked his head toward the closed door to his left. Based on the wailing, the girl that Lautaro Fernandez's men had kidnapped waited in the other room.

"You two going to stand here and chat or finish the rescue?" Ryan asked.

Reece scuffed the toe of his cowboy boot on the ground. "Your temperament is better suited to kids than mine, Walsh."

"All you have to do is walk in there and reassure her that she's safe and the police are coming."

Reece gave him a blank stare.

"Unbelievable." Ryan shook his head as he stalked toward the door.

Reece didn't like anything having to with kids and sickness, or kids and violence. He couldn't stand to see them suffer. Perhaps that was one of the reasons he'd never considered having any of his own. If he entered that room and discovered the men on the floor had harmed the young girl, he was liable to put a bullet in each of them.

Shooting people created entirely too much paperwork.

"Hello? Is this thing on?" Claire spoke into the com piece in his ear. Her role was IT support for Rider Security and Investigation where Reece, Santino, and Ryan worked. She'd been the one who'd identified the location of this hideout.

"We're here, Claire," Santino said.

"Is Reece going to stand around and chat us up with his Southern drawl, or is anybody frisking the bodies before the police arrive?" she asked. "This is a rescue mission, but may I remind you that we also need to learn more about this drug on the streets that got the DEA agent's daughter kidnapped in the first place?"

Santino bent down and began searching the men's pockets. From the other room, the kidnapped victim's wails stopped—clear proof that Ryan had been the right man to approach her. Aside from having a stepson who loved him like a father, Ryan Walsh had a calming ambience. Most people underestimated how deadly he could be.

Reece's phone buzzed with an alert. He pulled it out of the inside pocket of his leather jacket and activated the app that had alarmed. "What the hell?"

"Ah, ah," Santino scolded him. "That's another quarter in the jar."

"Somebody is breaking into Jess's apartment." Reece watched a man on-screen picking the lock to her room. His face was turned away from the motion-activated camera.

"I thought you and Jess broke up... again."

"We're merely on a temporary hiatus," he lied. The last breakup had been so distressingly awful, Reece worried it might have been their last.

Santino rifled through one of the men's wallets. "Right. So if you're not together, why are you still monitoring her place?"

"I don't expect one so young and inexperienced with relationships to comprehend my motives." He continued to watch the screen in disbelief as the man picked the lock and entered the apartment. A second man came into view of the camera, following the first and closing the door behind them.

"*Cualquiera*." Santino, who at twenty-eight was twelve years younger than Reece, rolled his eyes as he continued to check pockets. "Is she in danger?"

"She's not home at present, but," Reece checked his watch, "she will be in forty-five minutes if she doesn't make any stops after her shift."

Reece dialed Jess's mobile number, intending to warn her about the intruder. Of course, it went to voice mail. He wondered if she'd programmed her phone to silence his calls—wouldn't be the first time. He'd once had to use Rider resources to track her down at Nordstrom for a conversation.

"Call me, it's important." He disconnected the call.

Santino began frisking the next man on the floor. "If you need to go look out for your *not*-girlfriend who you're stalking through a door monitor, *vamos*. Ryan and I will clean up here."

"Take the car," Claire said in his earpiece. "I'll have Drake drive a new one to Ryan and Santino."

"Thanks, Claire." As Reece dashed to the car, he tried calling Jess again.

No answer. Damn stubborn woman.

His stomach churned at the thought of anything happening to her. He'd installed the motion detector for her after they'd had an argument where he told her she needed a safer place to live. A few months later, she'd told him she'd deleted the app from her phone because it triggered with every resident, delivery person, and dog walking down the hall. He'd then adjusted the settings so the alarm would only trigger for objects longer than five seconds in view, but by that time, they were taking another relationship break, so he doubted she'd reinstalled the app.

He drove in haste, palms sweating on the wheel as his heart raced, filled with worry and dread for Jess.

2

*B*one-deep fatigue settled into Jess after her night shift. Still, she preferred nights to days. Nighttime afforded a different level of camaraderie with the staff. There were no administrators lurking around, no Joint Commission visits to cite staff infractions, and no busy overhead announcements. At night, there was only her and the ICU team treating patients.

Medicine at its purist.

She drove her Tesla to her apartment mostly on autopilot as she thought about the acute lung injury—ALI—patient. Investigative diagnostics in the ICU were challenging mental gymnastics ... up to a point. Eventually, families wanted a prognosis, which would require a definitive diagnosis.

Currently, it was six a.m. in Chicago, but Jess called her friend Lori Sullivan anyway. The woman was single with no kids, like Jess, so she wouldn't be interrupting either much needed sleep or an early morning routine. And where Jess at least had a social life, Lori entertained herself mostly with research as she climbed the ladder of her academic career.

Lori didn't answer. Ah, well, it was too early perhaps. Her phone app icon indicated she had voice messages, probably her mother who typically left three in a row if Jess didn't pick up. She could check those later when she wasn't so tired.

She pulled into the parking lot and noted the charging station was occupied. Grr. If she had her own place, she wouldn't have to vie for the plug to charge her car. As she parked in an open standard slot, she thought of the time Reece had told her to move to a safer place and had even gone so far as to show her one with more charging stations. After all the effort he'd expended and then the bickering his suggestion prompted, it had never once occurred to him to invite her to live with him.

She shrugged off hurt feelings and the absurd longing she felt for a man closed to her. She pined for no one.

Sitting in the car a moment, she caught up on social media—Facebook, Snapchat, WhatsApp, Instagram, Marco Polo, and others. She updated her status and made plans for enjoying the Atlanta nightlife next weekend.

Lastly, Jess popped over to LinkedIn where some of her colleagues posted their latest articles, research papers, or promotions. But the headline of an article someone had posted caught her attention: "Researcher Dr. Lori Sullivan Dies in Motor Vehicle Crash."

"Oh, Lori." With a sinking heart, Jess clicked on the link to read the article.

Lori had died on Interstate 90, reportedly driving too fast and texting through a construction zone. The article went on to describe how there were nearly eight hundred car accidents a day in the state of Illinois, and two fatalities a day from these crashes.

Jess felt an eerie chill—she had been intubating the acute lung injury patient and thinking about her friend at almost the same time Lori had recklessly driven to her death. She tried to remember if the woman had siblings or surviving parents.

After Jess dropped the phone in her purse, she exited the car and entered the key code to the apartment complex. The sun rose over the east horizon but was mostly obscured by a landscape of concrete and postmodern buildings. She looked forward to being able to enjoy the view through her balcony window. She wanted to get out of her scrubs, take a hot shower, and drink decaf green tea to settle her before bed.

As she walked through the lobby, she remembered the call she'd received from the landlord before work yesterday—mail overflowed her box and she needed to empty it. She diverged her course from the elevators and headed for the mail slots. As she shoveled the contents into her large pink purse, she yawned. Maybe she wouldn't need that tea to wind down.

After taking the elevator up to the sixth floor, she unlocked her door and let herself inside her apartment.

For an instant, she thought perhaps she'd walked into the wrong apartment. The living room was completely trashed— lamps knocked over, cabinet contents strewn on the floor, couch stuffing bursting through slashes in the red fabric. Her mouth went dry as fear prickled through her.

Frantically, she dove her hand into her purse to retrieve her phone, but it was buried beneath a mound of mail, and she only succeeded in giving herself a dozen paper cuts.

A beastly arm wrapped around her waist, and a hand closed over her mouth before she could scream.

She thrashed uselessly and balked at his stench of body odor, but the man had pinned one arm to her side, and her other hand was trapped inside her purse. As she squirmed, her fingers closed around a smooth, small cylinder.

"You're going to tell me exactly where the USB is, or I'm going to chop you into little pieces of sashimi."

Jess wanted to tell this pig her heritage was Chinese not Japanese, but it was all she could do to breathe through her nose around his sweaty palm.

He squeezed her so hard she thought he might break her ribs or crack her into pieces like a fortune cookie.

She needed to make her move before she blacked out.

When Reece saw Jess's blue Tesla parked in the lot, he swore. He hadn't arrived before her. Damn Atlanta traffic.

He parked in haste before running toward the door, spurned by fear and dread. If she'd walked in on an active robbery, she could be injured, or worse.

He'd debated calling the police on his drive, but his ego told him he would handle the situation better than they could. All due respect to the men in blue, but they were bound by certain protocols. Reece wasn't.

When the code to the external keypad of the building worked, he was grateful it hadn't been changed in the last few months. He sprinted to the elevator where he caught his breath as he waited, impatiently pressing the up button several times. He dialed Jess's number again—for the fifth time.

"You've reached Jessica's answering service. Leave a message."

He cursed and resisted the urge to bang his fist on the elevator doors. He readjusted his earpiece with Claire still on the other line in case he needed her help.

At last, the elevator arrived. As he rode to Jess's floor, he pulled his gun from the holster on his waist. Taking a steadying breath, he forced himself to be calm.

Battle mode.

Neutralize the threat.

Rangers lead the way.

By the time he reached Jess's apartment, he'd stepped through his fear and emerged, cold, on the other side.

Her door was open.

When her living room came into view, he saw both Jess and one of her attackers. She stood, backed into the far wall of her living room, clutching a bronze Chinese dragon candlestick like a weapon in one hand and her purse in the other.

She wore her custom-fitted navy-blue scrubs and clogs. Her black hair was disheveled, suggesting she'd already been in a tussle.

The intruder rubbed at red irritated eyes. A canister of mace lay on the carpet—along with all of Jess's other possessions.

Reece's enjoyed a brief moment of pride knowing she'd fought back. His entire surveillance of the situation took about three seconds as he silently entered the room behind the pepper-sprayed man. Reece kicked his boot firmly into the man's knee and heard the satisfying crunch of grating cartilage and snapping ligament.

The man screamed as he dropped to the floor, clutching his appendage.

Motion caught the corner of Reece's eye as a figure moved from the bedroom into the hallway. Reece dropped to one knee as he turned and fired. The other man returned fire, and the bullet embedded in the far wall. As the second attacker crumpled, Reece rolled out of his line of sight, toward Jess.

No further shots resounded. Reece didn't know if he'd landed a kill shot or not, but he needed to ensure the scene's safety before he checked on Jess. She looked terrified, but she was standing, and that was enough for now.

He crouched near the man whose knee he'd busted. "Face down, hands behind your back, or I will strategically place my next bullet in your kidney."

"Screw you," the man spat.

Reece stood and kicked the man in his face. He wouldn't actually kill an unarmed man.

"Jess, you think you can keep that dragon trained on him while I go introduce myself to his partner in crime?"

She nodded, clutching the decorative candlestick for dear life. "I got this." Her voice was shaky as she kept her eyes fixed on the man she'd maced. "I got this," she repeated with more conviction.

Reece moved toward the hallway and pressed against one wall. When he peered around the corner, he saw the man he'd shot in a heap on the floor.

"We can play this one of two ways, hoss. You toss your gun on down the hall, and I'll call an ambulance for you. Or, if you would prefer, I have eleven more bullets for you that only cost me seventy-six cents apiece ... and then I'll call a hearse for you instead."

He heard a clunk. When he peeked again, the man still sat on the floor, but the gun now lay ten feet in front of him.

"Call an ambulance," the man said with a groan.

Reece tapped his ear com. "Claire, you still with me?"

"Waiting with bated breath."

"I need an ambulance and local PD to Jess's place." He suspected everyone on this floor of the building had probably already called the police after the gunfire.

"On it."

He pulled a spare twist tie out of his pocket and cinched the shooter's hands together. Since the man had a bullet in one shoulder, Reece opted to tie his hands in front of him.

"You gotta stop the bleeding, man," the burglar pleaded.

"You tell me what you're doing here, and I'll think about it." Reece picked up the man's 9mm, removing the clip and the bullet in the chamber.

"We were supposed to find a USB the Asian chick had. That's all I know."

Reece walked back into the living room and secured the other man's hands behind his back. Jess hadn't moved from her spot, still brandishing the snarling dragon candlestick. He'd never seen Jess's place so trashed. She was probably as much in shock from the destruction of her tidy home as from being attacked.

After he inspected the remainder of the apartment and was satisfied that no more surprises lurked in any other rooms, he returned to the bleeding man who was leaning, pale-faced, against one wall. Reece pressed a towel he'd grabbed off the kitchen floor against the wound.

"And did you discover what you were after?" Reece asked the injured man.

"I don't know."

Reece scrutinized the man's expression at his odd answer. While bleeding onto Jess's floor, the intruder broke eye contact and looked away at one corner.

As Reece knelt beside the burglar and applied pressure with the towel, the man grimaced. Reece dug into the man's right front shirt pocket and withdrew five USB drives. The man hadn't lied. He truly didn't know if he'd found the data source or not. It might or might not have been one of these, and he'd simply intended to steal all the USBs in hopes one of them was the one his boss sought.

Reece tucked them into the side of his boot. "Who hired you?"

The man pursed his lips and glared at him.

Reece pressed the barrel of his gun into the towel stuck to the guy's shoulder. He wasn't in the habit of torturing people, but he had a limited amount of time to get information before the police arrived.

He screamed. "Lautaro Fernandez!"

Surprise struck Reece at the name, but he kept his focus on the task at hand. "What's on the flash drive?"

"I don't know."

Reece gestured as though he would press the wound again.

"I don't know!"

Jess stormed down the hall, passing the pair of them. Reece stood and followed her. In her bedroom, she began throwing clothes into a suitcase.

"You okay?" He knew it was a stupid question, but he hadn't been gifted with Ryan Walsh's talent for soothing civilians after physical or emotional trauma. Of course she wasn't okay. She'd just had a break-in. He wanted to gather her in his arms and give her reassurance, but they hadn't exactly parted amicably after their last break up. She probably didn't want his hands on her any more than the beast she'd pepper-sprayed.

"I can't stay here." Her ears burned red, and she didn't make eye contact as she stuffed clothing and toiletries into the suitcase.

Was she packing for a European expedition with all those clothes?

"We have to stay for police questioning. After that, you can stay at my place."

She whirled on him. "I don't know what kind of shit show you've dragged me into, but I don't want any part of it."

"Hold on a damn minute, darling." The familiar quick flare of his temper ignited when arguing with her. No one could anger him from zero to sixty like this woman. "You think I'm responsible for these two clowns attacking you? Because I'd like to know how you're involved with an Argentinian drug lord."

Jess gaped at him—part incredulity, part anger. Reece couldn't decide if he wanted to shake the information out of her or kiss her into submission.

"Atlanta PD, put your hands above your head!"

3

———

"We have a situation."

Mica looked up from her computer screen at her employee who sported a deep burgundy bob, a T-shirt that said "I'm too techy for my shirt," and yoga pants. Her wide eyes of worry would have set Mica on high alert, but Claire was known to be a bit excitable.

"The Tuder case?" Mica asked. "Please don't tell me something bad happened to that DEA agent's daughter before we got there."

"No. She's fine. Ryan and Santino are with her, and the criminals are going to be arrested."

Mica sat up straighter. "Ryan and Santino? What about Reece?" She'd sent a three-man team in against two drug-dealing scum amateurs. Surely, no harm had befallen the third Rider employee.

"Reece had to go rescue Jess." Claire began to pace the length of Mica's office.

"Jess? As in Dr. Jessica Ong? Jenna's friend and Reece's girlfriend?"

"Um. Ex-girlfriend." Claire bit her lip.

"I can't keep up." Mica stood and stretched. She adjusted the photo of her and her husband David on her desk. "They're on-again off-again more than Justin Timberlake and Jessica Biel before they finally got married."

"Yes. Well, anyway, some men broke into Jess's apartment, and she came home after work while they were ransacking her place."

"That's scary. Is she okay?" Mica knew Jess was a physician. She didn't recall her having any self-defense training. Reece probably would have given her some—unless training day fell on one of their off-again months.

"She's okay. And the police are at her place now."

"Good."

"The thing is," Claire wrung her hands together as she balanced on the balls of her feet, "this wasn't a regular B and E. They were looking for a specific USB drive."

"Why?"

"We don't know, but the burglars also work for Lautaro Fernandez."

Mica ran a hand through her ear-length blonde hair, trying to follow the complexity of the situation. "What does Reece's ex-girlfriend have on an electronic storage drive that a drug dealer would want?"

"I don't know. Can I start digging?" Claire asked.

"You want to open a case file?"

"Yes. For Reece."

"Hmm." Mica pursed her lips. "Start digging, but we'll make it unofficial for now, in the event that this was some sort of mistaken identity."

"Okay."

"In case it's more serious, do Reece and Dr. Ong have plans to lay low for a while?"

"Reece's place has security and weapons," Claire offered.

Mica pulled her phone out of her pocket. "I'll text him and remind him that he can use my father's cabin if he wants to be a little further off the grid."

She began texting as Claire left to do her electronic digging.

A knock came at the door. "Claire—" But she stopped when she saw a balding man with gray hair. "Dad, this is a pleasant surprise." She sent the text to Reece and pocketed her phone.

"Hey, baby girl."

She came around the desk and gave him a hug. "What brings you downtown?"

"Business. I had to drop off a Shelby Ford Mustang to a customer, so I thought I'd pop by while in the neighborhood. How's the munchkin?"

"Allen is good. David is off today, so he's watching him."

Her father lifted the photo off the desk of her and David—husband and wife. "You should go virtual. Lots of companies are doing it—everyone working from home with no central office. You could be with Allen more and not have the overhead of this office."

"Sometimes I consider it. Sometimes an old-fashioned part of me wants an office and reception area."

"How are the Alonso twins doing?" He set the photo back down.

"Excellent."

Mica's father had been the one to suggest the hires. After she'd done extensive background checks and interviews, she'd given them the job. So far, they were not only competent in security—offense and defense—but they were amicable with the other team members.

"Santino is working with Reece and Ryan. Rafe is on his way to South America for a little recon."

Her father raised his eyebrows. "Sounds serious."

"We just rescued a DEA agent's daughter from an Argentinian drug lord. We need more information. Also, Bill Sharp's daughter is down there. She won't let us put official protection on her, but her father asked that we lurk within her proximity. The weapons developer has his share of enemies."

"The twins do okay working apart?"

"No problems so far. Oh, family holiday photos this weekend. Don't forget."

"I won't. On a side note, I've been working on something for the Rider team—a prototype."

She blinked at him, unsure where the conversation was headed, but since he was retired military and now worked on cars, she assumed he was mixing the two. The thought worried her.

"Souped-up Humvees," he said. "Complete with defensive and offensive measures. It's still a work in progress. Might be done in another month or so."

Mica chuckled nervously. "What'd you do? Put a rocket launcher on one?" When he only grinned, she gaped. "Seriously, Dad? You weaponized a street vehicle? That's illegal."

He snorted. "Half of the things your company does are illegal. Besides, I worry about all those bad guys you and your team face."

So did she. "What do you want from me?" she asked, part interest, part dread.

He grinned as if she'd just offered to spring for his favorite ice cream. "Test-drive her after the holidays. Tell me what you think." He started walking toward the door.

She frowned. "I prefer to solve cases with discretion—not rocket launchers from Humvees."

"As history has demonstrated, some of the foes you face can't be managed discretely."

Jess stared out the window as Reece drove her car to some undisclosed location. Exhaustion tugged at her eyelids, and Reece at the wheel was a relief.

He'd confiscated her cell phone after the police questioning had concluded. After he activated her car with it, he'd turned it off. As such, she had no internet to distract her from her thoughts.

The two of them hadn't yet spoken about how they'd accused each other of being the cause of the break-in at her apartment. She'd overheard one of the attackers tell Reece they were supposed to collect a USB drive, even though they'd later told the police they planned to steal jewelry and her designer purses. Since Reece hadn't mentioned the storage drives he'd taken from the injured man to the police, Jess had kept her mouth shut about them too. Nothing made sense, and she was worn out from working all night and answering questions from the police all morning.

"I don't know anything about any Argentinian drug dealers." She finally broke the silence between them, her tone carrying all the fatigue that was weighing her down.

"Those men were hired by Lautaro Fernandez to steal a USB drive from you."

"Yes, I overheard the one you shot when you were torturing him. My USBs have photos and videos of my trips—Thailand, Iceland, and Singapore. Hardly worth risking going to jail over— or getting shot." One collection comprised all photos of her and Reece—cozy and comfortable. They'd had some amazing times together. She glanced at him and the familiar silhouette of a strong jaw, broad nose, and generous lips. Between the latter two was a thick mustache. She used to enjoy the feel of coarse hairs on her neck when he kissed her. He had brown hair down to his ears, where the strands curled slightly. He almost always wore blue jeans and cowboy boots unless work called for a suit, in which case he still wore cowboy boots. Her friend Jenna had once likened him to Wyatt Earp, but Jess felt he was more of a Doc Holliday or, even more apt; Timothy Olyphant from his role in *Justified*.

"Any chance you saw something you weren't supposed to see on one of your trips?" Reece asked.

"Not that I know of." She turned to look back out the window.

"Perhaps you caught someone on camera who didn't want to be seen."

She shrugged. "Most of them are just beautiful scenery."

"Maybe your boyfriend left his USB drive at your place and this is his fault."

She shot a sidelong look at Reece. She had moved from Chicago to Atlanta for Reece, only to have the relationship crash and burn several times.

"No." And she left it at that. The last thing she would do is give him the satisfaction of knowing she hadn't dated anyone else since their breakup. "If this Argentinian dickhead really is after me and this is unrelated to your company, how did you know to come save me?"

"Is that a thank-you?" he asked.

She hadn't thanked him. She'd been so relieved to see him initially that her heart had soared and her fear took a momentary hiatus. Despite their rocky past, she'd known he would protect her. But then she'd thought he was perhaps the one who had put her in danger in the first place. Now, she didn't know what to think.

"Maybe..." she replied.

"All my efforts are worth a measly 'maybe'?" His voice had a teasing tone.

"I can't even think straight, and you didn't answer my question."

He shifted in the driver's seat. "I will answer your question if you permit me to answer it in its entirety before you decide to get cross with me."

She folded her arms. "Okay."

"You were dissatisfied with the sensitivity of your motion sensor outside your apartment door. I reset it for you, but I still needed to test it. Since you weren't willingly communicating with me at the time, I loaded the app on my phone. As such, this morning, when you had an intruder, I was alerted to his presence."

Jess shuddered at the mention of the intruder. A cold sensation ran through her bones. If Reece hadn't gifted her that industrial strength mace, she wouldn't have freed herself from the smelly man's grasp. And if Reece hadn't arrived in the nick of time, those men would be demanding to know the location of a USB drive that she knew nothing about.

A thank-you began to form on her lips.

And if she and Reece were still together, she might never have been in danger. She clamped her mouth shut, no longer feeling a thank-you was in order.

"When we get to the safehouse, you can use my phone. Is there anyone you need to call when we get there?"

She understood he was implying her phone might be traced, although that seemed impossible, since she never let it out of her sight. Her friend Jenna had even accused Jess's phone of being another vital organ—one Jess wouldn't survive without.

She shook her head. "My next shift is in four days. I just finished seven on."

"Family or friends?"

"No." She wanted to talk to Jenna, but she was still working her day shift in the ICU.

The other reason Jess hadn't wanted to call her friend was because Jess refused to cry in front of Reece. Jenna—having been through quite an ordeal herself a few years ago—would be empathic, which would cause Jess to break down into tears. As a Ranger turned private security, Reece probably didn't tolerate weakness, and the last thing she wanted to do was give him a reason to lose even more respect for her. He already took her for some type of "powder puff"—descriptive words he'd specifically used during one of their heated arguments—because she dressed fashionably.

How many times had he frowned at the sight of her high heels? If he was five feet tall, he'd wear four-inch heels too. Instead, he was over six feet of lean, sinewy muscle. She'd loved the way he used to bend to her level, wrap his arms around her, and lift her to him for a kiss. So much emotion had been revealed in all that effort.

But they were finished. They'd said as much during their last quarrel. Besides, she had bigger problems. She needed to understand what the thieves had been after, and why.

Judging by the fact that armed men were breaking into her house, her life might depend on discovering the truth.

"WHAT DO YOU MEAN SHE DISAPPEARED?" Lautaro Fernandez demanded into the phone on speaker mode.

"After I heard the police had been called to Dr. Ong's apartment, I went there myself. She's gone, and our men have been arrested. I'm told a white man in cowboy boots took down our men. I don't know where the physician went—*desapareció como polvo en el viento.*"

Lautaro cursed. The job had been sloppy to begin with, but they'd been in a rush to intercept the USB. He paced near the window of his condo at Lenox Square. From his view, he could see the mall and his favorite sushi restaurant.

His gaze slid back to the phone. The physician lived alone; they'd had no reason to expect a man to arrive, much less one who could debilitate Lautaro's men. Had Dr. Sullivan somehow warned Dr. Ong, or had it been chance? *Mala seurte?*

Lautaro had sent the best men he'd had available on short notice, but they'd been handicapped by a deadline and insufficient time to plan. He couldn't afford to kill Dr. Ong, in the event that they needed to question her about the location of the USB. Now, he had two men out of commission—one shot and one arrested by the police.

And who the hell knew what was on the *maldito* USB? All Lautaro had been told was that the information in the hands of the authorities would be the end of his lucrative business partnership. He had enough financial incentive not to ask questions and just retrieve the storage drive.

Except now he was empty-handed—no USB and no Dr. Ong. Lautaro had to report this failure to Mr. Shoup, but that didn't mean Lautaro had to stop working to find the physician. She might have vanished like dust in the wind as the caller had suggested, or she might have just crawled under a rock they needed to overturn.

"Are you still there?" Lautaro asked.

"*Si, señor.*"

"Find out exactly what happened at Dr. Ong's apartment. Question our men. Then, start looking into her friends and family so we can determine who she would run to."

"*Si, señor* Fernandez."

He hung up the phone as a knock sounded at his door.

"*Entras!*" Lautaro called out.

Mateo entered, followed by Lautaro's brother, Dom. Mateo sported a suit, dressing sharp as Lautaro preferred. Dom wore baggy jeans and a Che Guevara T-shirt. Unlike Lautaro's smoothly shaven face, Dom had untidy patches of scruff. Lautaro's face twitched in irritation. His brother was part of a billion-dollar organization—he could try to dress the part rather than looking like a derelict.

Mateo held his electronic tablet in one hand, ready to discuss business matters. Dom dropped onto the office couch like he hadn't a care in the world. Perhaps he didn't, since all of the pressure of the business fell on Lautaro's shoulders.

Mateo ran through details of shipments and deliveries. Nothing had been raided or seized, so perhaps kidnapping the DEA agent's daughter had temporarily served its purpose.

"Lastly, *señor*," Mateo said, "there is report of a dock manager who stole some inventory."

Lautaro rubbed irritably at his right eyebrow. Mateo always saved the bad news for last in case it was severe enough for Lautaro to lose his temper—a demon below the surface who threatened to claw his way out.

"This thief is gone or no?"

"No, *señor*. We have him in custody."

Lautaro sat at his desk and organized loose papers. "We have protocols for this. Why are you bothering me with it? Retaliate. Kids or wife, I don't care."

"He has neither, *señor*."

"Sister? Brother?"

Mateo shook his head.

Lautaro narrowed his eyes at his assistant. "That was a poor hire by HR, then. We hire people who have something to lose. It's how they're kept in line."

"An oversight, I'm sure."

"Fine. Did we reacquire whatever he attempted to steal?"

"*Si. Cien kilos de heroina.*"

"Then kill him. Send a message about what we do to thieves."

4

Reece would not have deemed the silence in the car ride comfortable, but at least Jess wasn't biting his head off. Yet her silence worried him. Jess was energetic and feisty, like Hunan spicy beef. If she was subdued, it usually meant something dark lurked beneath the surface.

He wanted to offer words of reassurance, but he was probably the last person she wanted to see in the middle of a crisis—much less talk to. Eventually, she would have to discuss the situation with him, because he had every intention of being on the forefront of discovering exactly what those men sought and why.

The phone in his pocket buzzed repeatedly as he drove. Probably half the Rider team was calling or texting him about the incident. They'd just have to wait. Reece would only further unnerve Jess if he talked in front of her, and he wouldn't text while driving—even though Jess's Tesla had automatic pilot. He trusted the car, but he didn't trust all the other morons on the road.

When at last they arrived at the secluded cabin in the North Georgia mountains, he parked in the drive close to the front.

Jess followed him to the porch. She carried a gargantuan pink bag she referred to as her purse, and he carried her overstuffed suitcase, which probably would have exceeded cargo weight limits for a commercial airline flight.

He didn't care if he had to lug her entire apartment here. Jess was safe, and that was all that mattered.

As soon as he punched in the key code and opened the door, she strode past him, dropping her purse on the kitchen table. "Shower?"

"You can have the bedroom down the hallway on the left."

"Thank you." Her gratitude was thick with sincerity and exhaustion. She took the suitcase handle from him and wheeled it down the hall.

She hadn't slept in almost twenty-four hours, so he expected her to crash in the bed after her shower. In case she didn't—owing to lingering adrenaline or just perpetual anger at him—he pulled out a mug and added water.

Next, he used his secure phone to call Ryan Walsh.

"Reece, what the hell? You take off before our case is wrapped up, and I hear from Claire that Jess is in trouble."

"There wasn't time to explain. But she's not presently in danger. We're at the safehouse." He ruffled through an assortment of tea. No decaf green tea. She'd have to settle for chamomile.

"What happened?" Ryan asked.

"Two unscrupulous gentlemen in Lautaro Fernandez's employment broke into Jess's apartment. They were searching for a USB drive they believe is in her possession."

"And Claire said Jess arrived home while they were still there?"

"Yes. Thanks to her pepper spray, her quick thinking, and a rather intimidating candlestick with a pointy tail, she kept the men at bay until I arrived." He set the tea bag beside the teacup and placed the honey next to it.

"She's okay?"

"She is uninjured. 'Okay' might be a stretch."

"Did the burglars get the storage drive they were after?"

"I have in my possession all of the USBs from her apartment at the time of the robbery, and the two criminals are in police custody." Fortunately, when the police took Reece's gun into evidence and frisked him, they didn't make him remove the boot where he'd stashed the USBs. "Whether or not one of these half dozen drives is the culprit remains to be determined."

Ryan said, "I'll send Santino to you and get him to bring some groceries. Maybe he can bring the flash drives back for Claire to analyze."

Reece stayed silent a beat.

His partner sighed. "I'm sorry. I would come myself, but when Claire said Lautaro Fernandez was behind the attack, my first thought was that he could be targeting our loved ones. I'm waiting here to make sure Jenna gets home safe. I'll join you as soon as I can."

Reece stroked his mustache. Enemies had targeted Rider SI in the past, so Ryan's fear was justified. Reece had been initially disappointed that Ryan—his best friend and work partner—wasn't rushing to Reece's aid, but Reece would have stayed with Jess if roles were reversed.

"You did the right thing, Walsh," Reece assured him. "And you should remain in the company of your wife. Jess and Jenna are best friends. Since the burglars didn't procure the information they sought from Jess's place, Jenna could become a target."

"I feel like I'm leaving you hanging."

"Not at all. We're safe. The only thing you would accomplish by being here is watching Jess glare at me."

The other man grunted. "You saved her, and she's still mad at you? That must have been a bad breakup."

"The woman has mastered the art of holding a grudge."

"Good luck. And keep me posted."

After concluding his conversation with Ryan, Reece started a fire in the large living room fireplace and poured himself a glass of whiskey. The afternoon sun shone through dense pines and the bare branches of poplar and oak.

He sank down into the couch, pulled off his boots, and set the flash drives on the lamp table to his right. Leaning back, he propped his feet on the coffee table.

Jess emerged from the back room with dark, wet hair and dressed in silk pajamas. Reece remained still and averted his eyes, staring at the fire as he listened to her pad over to the kitchen. He felt a trickle of satisfaction when the microwave's beeps and hums indicated she was making the tea he'd left out for her.

He waited silently as golden flames danced before his eyes. Would she retreat to her room for much needed sleep? Did she want to talk about what happened at her apartment? Since he had possession of her power-downed phone in case it was being monitored, Reece was the only person available for her to talk to right now.

But he wouldn't push, not this afternoon when she needed rest. Tomorrow he would.

She brought the tea over and sat on the end of the couch, two feet from him. Curling into a ball, she drank her tea and watched the fire with him.

"You were impressive back there at my apartment. The way you handled those men..." She shuddered as her voice trailed off.

"I've had an abundance of training and experience. I'm certain if I ever saw you manage an ICU patient and save a life, I would be equally impressed."

She quietly drank her tea again, hopefully thinking of the ICU and not the burglars.

Reece reached for her slowly and drew her foot to him. She surrendered to the familiar gesture and repositioned her feet to rest in his lap. She set her tea on the table. When he began to massage, he remembered how this had been their routine—she would finish a twelve-hour shift and he would be there to help her relax.

They'd had a good thing, until he'd screwed it up.

As he rubbed her feet, the tension visibly eased out of her body. Normally, this was the part where she'd talk about her day.

"Thank you." She closed her eyes and didn't speak another word.

When Reece was certain her slow breaths were indicative of deep slumber, he scooped her up in his arms and carried her to bed. After tucking her in, he left the room. He kept quiet, though he knew from experience the woman could sleep through noise equivalent to a Chinese New Year festival.

He smelled the faint scent of jasmine in the air and smiled. He'd missed her smell. Missed the feel of her petite body in his arms.

But the issues that had driven them apart hadn't dissolved just because a crisis had surfaced. They were still two very different people.

Back in the kitchen, he plugged both their phones into the wall chargers. Next, he dug Jess's laptop out of her purse and copied the data from the many USB drives onto the computer.

The late afternoon sun began to dip. The day had ebbed away during the several hours they'd spent in police questioning, followed by Atlanta traffic as they drove north to this location, then Jess's long shower and winding down.

Headlights shone down the driveway and into the living room. Reece assumed the arrival was Santino, since only the Rider team knew about the safehouse, but he would still take precautions.

He'd had to surrender his discharged weapon to Atlanta PD as evidence after he shot the intruder; fortunately, the cabin had its own source of firepower.

From a bookshelf in the living room, he retrieved a hollowed out hardback edition of *War and Peace* and withdrew the 9mm stored there. He checked the clip before slipping it into the holster under his jacket.

A knock came from the door. "It's Santino."

In a few long strides, Reece arrived at the door and peeked through the glass, confirming the presence of his rookie partner.

When he opened the door, Santino was loaded down with groceries. He carried the paper bags into the kitchen as Reece closed and locked the door.

"You were careful?" Reece asked.

"I know the protocols, man. No one followed me here."

"Thanks for the groceries." Reece began helping store the food.

Santino snorted. "I thought it would be a simple pickup, but then Ryan calls me and says Jenna wants to make sure I know that Jess is lactose intolerant and doesn't drink alcohol. So, I'm like, there goes my wine-and-cheese idea. Omelet? Nope, not that either."

"Your selection looks just fine." Reece stored eggs and other perishables in the refrigerator. He set the box of green tea off to the side on the counter.

"So, what's the story?" Santino asked.

"We've yet to peruse the USB drives and discover the source of interest."

"Your girlfriend is okay though?"

"Not my girlfriend."

Santino's lips quirked. "The way you dashed to her rescue like a knight in shining armor suggests she's more than a casual romantic interest."

Jess had certainly been more than casual. Reece had never felt about a woman the way he felt about Jess. But deep passion didn't automatically make two people compatible—as evidenced by their many breakups.

"Are there any more groceries to fetch from your car?" Reece asked, not bothering to disguise the irritation in his voice in order to appropriately convey that the topic of Jess and him was off-limits.

"No. You want me to stay or go?"

"I want you to *deliver*. I have copied the Jess's USB data to her laptop. This way, she can look at the data here while you take the USBs to Claire for analysis. The first step to securing Jess's safety is to learn what information is hidden there."

"Why not just send them to Claire in a zip drive over the internet?"

"The wireless service is too slow out here for the many gigabytes of data likely on those drives, and I'd rather leave the system turned off and keep us off the grid as long as possible until this situation is resolved."

Jess sat up in bed and blinked her eyes open. She looked around the room as the morning sun cast a surreal glow through the bare trees outside her window. On taupe walls hung paintings of bear and elk near a river deep within a forest. The imagery mimicked how she felt—turbulent and cold as some unknown fate swept her into a dark abyss.

But she had Reece—the man who'd swooped in and rescued her. The same man who'd broken her heart.

She smelled the scent of eggs in the air.

The man who was cooking breakfast.

She ran a comb through her hair before heading to the kitchen. Once upon a time, she had to be entirely presentable before she'd greet him in the morning, but their relationship had advanced beyond that at some point. This morning, she was too starved to care if he saw her in her pajamas with no makeup.

"Morning, sunshine." Reece wore jeans and a T-shirt. His leather jacket lay over one of the counter barstools.

She breathed deeply of the scent of food. "That smells so good."

Reece grinned, and a familiar warmth spread through Jess. He slid a cup of tea over to her, and she was grateful to have something other than him to stare at, though she still felt his gaze on her.

At last, he turned and resumed cooking—stirring vegetables into a skillet of scrambled eggs.

She drank the tea, which was at the perfect temperature, suggesting he'd heated the water when he'd heard her stirring in the bedroom.

"Any new information about my break-in?" Jess inquired.

Reece's company had resources to investigate criminal activity. Jess had even met their computer guru, Claire Maltisse, at a girls' night out with Mica, who ran Rider SI, and her longtime physician friend, Jenna.

"You want to talk shop before breakfast?" He kept his back to her as he cooked, but his tone sounded tentative.

"Yes, shoptalk." She needed to solve this problem now so her life could hopefully return to normal. Normal meant no heartache with Reece around. Well, less heartache.

In the meantime, she would keep her dignity and self-respect. "I'll hire the Rider team. I'd like to have Claire see what she can uncover." Jess was a career woman. She'd take handouts from no one.

Reece stiffened slightly as he seasoned the eggs. "I'm sure Mica can review the cost structure with you. That's not my area of expertise."

Jess recalled the way Reece had taken down the two intruders —one as large as The Rock and the other armed with a gun. Yesterday, for the first time, she'd witnessed Reece's area of expertise.

She dipped her tea bag up and down in the warm water, watching the greenish-golden color darken. "I clearly also need your expertise." As hard as it would be to have him close, she had to admit she felt safer with him around.

But she respected herself too much to beg. If he needed to excuse himself from her case for personal reasons, she'd hire someone else from Rider Security and Investigation. Ryan Walsh had protected Jenna spectacularly. Or there was Billy Parrish, who could keep pace with Jess's cussing and had great listening skills. Oh, and what about the new guys? The Alonso twins. They weren't as experienced as the other Rider members, but they would probably be zealous in their efforts to prove themselves to the rest of the team.

Reece turned and placed a Southwest breakfast burrito before her. Because he'd fixed it, she knew the dish would have lactose-free cheese.

"I am at your disposal."

His words danced along her skin. He'd put no stipulation on his commitment. Not "at your disposal *for the duration of your investigation*." Not "at your disposal *as it pertains to your investigation*." And if more words could be used to add stipulations and clarity, Reece would use them.

Or Jess could be reading too much into his statement.

"Thank you." She picked up the burrito and took a bite.

"Santino came by yesterday and took your USBs to courier them to Claire for analysis. I copied them onto your laptop first, though, so you can review the contents."

She glanced at the table where her purse and laptop rested. At some point, she'd shared her password with Reece while they'd been dating. Apparently, he'd remembered it.

He continued as she ate, "Claire will no doubt have been burning the midnight oil to find a connection between anything on your flash drives and the Argentinian drug dealer."

"I'm grateful." The faster everyone worked, the faster the investigation would be over. "Tell me. How bad is this Lautaro character?"

Reece frowned.

"That bad?" she asked. "Bad like *Terminator* bad?"

He leaned on the counter. "Bad like *No Country for Old Men* Anton Chigurh bad."

She swallowed. "Oh." They'd watched that movie together, and she'd found the sociopath's utter lack of conscience terrifying.

"Rumor has it there were three Fernandez brothers and Lautaro was the middle child who eliminated the firstborn in order to take over the Argentinian cartel."

Jess wrung her hands together. "You know, you really shouldn't sugarcoat these things for me." Her joke fell flat.

"Do you need to make arrangements with your work schedule?" Reece asked.

"I'm due back in three days. You tell me. How long does solving a case like this typically take?" She savored another bite of burrito.

His mustache twitched with an amused quirk of his lips. "Darling, there is nothing typical about any of the cases we work. Six days to six months."

"Ever solved one in three days?" The full stomach and delicious tea had raised her spirits enough to ask hopefully

"We will strive to our utmost ability, but I cannot make promises I'm uncertain we can deliver upon."

"That's okay. I know I've got the best. I have the team who rescued a tennis star from a psychotic Russian physician, saved my best friend from her ex-husband's twelve-million-dollar mistake with the Cuban mafia, took down a crooked security company, and protected one of America's top rock stars. It takes as long as it takes."

Reece swiped her empty plate and moved it to the sink.

Jess took her tea and relocated it next to her laptop, where she began looking at the contents of the USB drives. The sooner they solved the mystery of what prize information lurked in those electronic files, the sooner the fear nibbling at the frayed edges of her mind would subside.

5

When his friend Ryan Walsh called, Reece used the opportunity to step outside the cabin. He needed to distance himself from Jess—her petite body in that silk nightgown with all of her long, dark hair and gorgeous, smooth skin was more than a little distracting.

He pulled on his jacket. "Walsh," Reece greeted him.

"How is Jess?"

"Small package, lots of fortitude. She's scrutinizing all of her storage drives now to see if anything can be linked to Lautaro." Reece walked the length of the driveway and paced. His breath condensed in the crisp December air and his cheeks chilled.

"How are you holding up?"

"She asked about purchasing Rider services," Reece said grimly. "If that's not a line in the sand, I don't know what is."

"She's not a mind reader. You broke things off. You've told *me* you regretted it, but she doesn't know that."

Reece grunted as he kicked at a fallen branch on the side of the driveway.

Ryan continued, enunciating his words carefully, "So maybe it's a line in the sand, or maybe she's trying to respect what you do as a profession."

"Be that as it may, we have a case to close. Is it too soon to inquire about updates?" The bucking bronco in him wanted to go after Lautaro himself. Battling criminals would allow Reece to focus his thoughts away from the beautiful woman in the cabin with him—but first they needed to understand the drug dealer's motives.

"Claire's been working all night."

"Bless her," Reece said.

"Give her a call, and she'll tell you what she knows."

"I'll be in touch."

"Reece?"

"Yeah."

"Can I honestly tell my wife her best friend is okay?" Ryan asked.

"Jess is as tough as a bull rider and defended herself capably before I was on the scene. This morning, she's all business. You tell Jenna she's okay. She'll call her later, and I'm not letting danger near her again."

When he finished his call with Ryan, Reece called Claire.

"I owe you, Claire."

"I know." Her voice was chipper—not a tone most people could pull off after a long night of research. But she was in her element helping people remotely through her computer skills. "You may be less grateful when I tell you I've come up empty."

"We always accept that detective work is ninety-nine percent excluding things in order to uncover the truth."

"I scoured all of Jess's stored photos—nothing suspicious. If some random person was caught in her background, facial recognition didn't pick them up."

He wondered if this entire debacle could be a case of mistaken identity, but he doubted that.

Claire continued, "Not yet anyway, I'm still running some of them. Most of the photos are of her with friends—social butterfly that she is. Many others are of the two of you." She let the last sentence hang.

"Uh-huh."

"Some are organized, you know, like she was going to create a printed album or scrapbook."

Reece cleared his throat. "Are you in possession of any additional information related to her situation?" He didn't want to ponder what it meant that Jess had kept photos of them. Maybe she just hadn't gotten around to deleting them.

"You two look good together," Claire said wistfully, as if she was gazing upon a photo as she spoke.

How much had Ryan Walsh blabbed to his pseudo-younger sister Claire about Reece's relationship? Ah, well, there were no secrets among the Rider SI family.

"Focus, Claire," he said.

"Sorry goes a long way," she pressed. "Plus, you rescued her. I forgave Drake."

Claire's husband Drake had lied about his undercover work when he and Claire were dating. After rescuing her from a kidnapping and completing a prerequisite amount of groveling, they'd made amends.

"Lautaro Fernandez," Reece spoke the words deliberately.

"Okay. Okay. We're going to put out some feelers underground and see what surfaces. Dorian has some old contacts, and Ryan will check with Ernesto Busta."

Reece recalled the Miami drug dealer whom Rider SI had dealings with a few years ago. Kingpins made it their business to know about the competition, so asking Ernesto was a solid move.

And since the Cuban American revered the former Russian mob leader Vladimir Pronin—now Mica's mother in-law's boyfriend—Ernesto might be forthcoming with information.

After his conversation with Claire, Reece walked back into the warmth of the cabin. He tried to give Jess space to work as he busied himself cleaning the kitchen, but he refreshed her tea twice out of some sophomoric desire to encroach on her space.

At last, she stood and stretched. He averted his eyes from the pale flesh of her abdomen, exposed as her shirt crept higher. He'd traced kisses along that sensitive skin once upon a time.

"Fabulous. Three hours later, and I still have no idea why somebody would want one of my USB drives." She pointed to the different flash drives sequentially as she spoke, "Pictures, pictures, random files I haven't sorted through in ten years, and a compilation of all my publications and abstracts." She cast a sad expression at the last USB.

"What was that look for?" Reece asked.

"What look?"

"You had this fleeting expression like your cat just died when you looked at your publications drive."

"I don't have a cat."

"Jess."

"Okay, but it was a selfish thought. One of the abstracts on the drive was a presentation a colleague of mine and I wrote on acute lung injury from a street drug. We were working on expanding it to a case series for publication in a journal."

"And the sad part?"

"I read online yesterday that my coauthor died in a car accident. She was a great physician and phenomenal researcher. Her loss is tragic. The thought crossing my mind was 'Shit, how do I write that paper if she's dead and can't sign the author agreement form?' Pretty selfish thing to think."

"Your first instinct wasn't to remove her from the paper, so you're not all bad." His mustache twitched.

"Gee, thanks." She scooped up her flash drives and dumped them in her purse while simultaneously knocking over the gargantuan pink bag.

The contents spilled across the table and onto the floor.

"Dammit," she swore on an exhale, scrambling after the items.

Leaflets of mail fanned out, along with a wallet, lipstick, Tic-Tacs, her hospital badge, a pack of tissues, a small hand sanitizer, nail polish, fingernail clippers, packets of instant coffee, tea bags, eyeliner, mascara, ponytail holders, and a knit hat.

"You could help," Jess snapped.

"I could." He licked his lips. "But the view from up here is much too nice." He glanced behind her as she crawled on her hands and knees.

Before she could call him any crass names, he chuckled and knelt to help. "I'm helping. I'm helping."

He picked up a *National News* magazine. "This is the one your brother writes for?" He flipped through the pages.

"Yeah, he sends me the issues when there's an article he wrote. I keep all of them."

Reece hadn't met her brother—or any of Jess's family—but he knew Jay worked as a reporter. He covered a variety of topics from global warming to human rights to political scandals. He saw Jay's article: "Asia Trade Deal Signed" by Jay Ong. A pressure intensified in Reece's chest at the memory of Jess's invitation to meet her family. He'd immediately proceeded to instigate a fight and caused their relationship to implode. Now, meeting her family seemed like an important way to mend what he'd damaged between them.

Jess suddenly went rigid and pale.

"What's wrong?" Reece asked.

She rocked back on her knees, grasping a padded manilla envelope. "Son of a bitch."

"Jess?"

She tore open an envelope and tipped the contents onto her palm. A single silver USB drive fell out. "My colleague sent this days before she died." Her voice was a dry whisper. "It must be what Lautaro's men were after."

JESS STARED at the USB drive in her hand as her heart thudded with a mixture of fear, reservation, and excitement. The answer to why she had been attacked lay in the palm of her hand, but she had a sinking feeling the truth could be as bad as not knowing. Opening the envelope wider, she peered inside and withdrew a note.

> *Jess,*
> *Call me when you get this, and I'll explain.*
> *—Lori*

Did this mean that Lori Sullivan's death wasn't accidental? Receiving this the day two men broke into Jess's apartment could not have been a coincidence. But what dealings did Lori have with a drug dealer, and why involve Jess?

"What was her explanation?" Reece asked, his expression one of concern as he tried to read the note over her shoulder.

She passed it to Reece so he could read it. "I don't know. Lori certainly didn't tell me she was mailing me anything. And now she can't even tell me why. What the hell kind of shit show did she drag me into?"

"Only one way to find out," Reece said.

Jess abandoned the rest of the cleanup and returned to the

laptop where she inserted the drive. She hesitated, feeling the weight of her colleague's death, understanding that the woman who had sent this to her was now gone.

"Password protected," Reece murmured.

"That's not a problem." Jess typed in the password. "We created one for sharing our work confidentially."

Reece leaned in close as she opened the file on the drive. She could smell his Armani aftershave—the one she'd bought him—and was bombarded with dozens of memories of their time together.

She sniffed and forced herself to remain focused on the spreadsheet before her. She stared at the rows and columns as she scrolled through words, acronyms, and numbers.

"You understand any of this?" Reece asked.

"Yes. 'ID' is the patient's assigned record number—used in order to avoid identifying patient information such as name or social security number. One row for each patient."

"So, the *M* and *F* are male or female, the next column is age and the next is ethnicity," he said.

"Right. Then there are the various lab work values and chest imaging findings—text with mostly medical acronyms."

"What is this one?" He pointed. "This column only has either ILL or TRL."

"I don't know. They aren't medical acronyms."

"Why would Dr. Sullivan send you a file of patient information?"

"This is our data. Well, some of it. I didn't think we had this many patients. She must have had other researchers also identifying patients."

Had she expanded the project to other investigators and not told Jess? How many other secrets did Lori take with her to the grave? Perhaps Jess was jumping to conclusions. Lori could have collected all this data herself. But why hadn't she mentioned sooner?

"And the purpose of this registry and your planned paper was to identify the respiratory complications of an illegal drug?" Reece asked.

She blinked at him.

"I do pay attention," he shot back.

She remembered him seeing her editing the abstract last year. "Yes. Luminous was the street name. We didn't know its composition but based on the urine drug screens in this data set, it's some type of narcotic—all the subjects had narcotics in their urine drug screen." She ran the cursor along the spreadsheet, highlighting the column that said "narcotics."

She rubbed her temples. "Maybe they all had side effects from Luminous? I'm feeling more and more like Lori's death wasn't an accident."

"You think perhaps Lautaro learned about Dr. Sullivan's investigative research?"

"Even if that happened, what does Lautaro care? Street drugs kill people all the time. What does a drug dealer care if a couple doctors write a paper in a low-tier journal about it? Narcotics can kill you—it's not exactly a news flash." She waved her hands in the air. "Fifty thousand people die every year in the US from opioid-involved overdoses. Fifteen thousand from heroin."

"We are obviously not in possession of all of the facts." Reece stroked his mustache before pulling out his phone.

Jess stared at the screen, baffled and terrified. What had her friend uncovered that resulted in her being murdered? And if Jess didn't figure it out, was she next?

"Claire," he began when his call connected. "I need everything you can unearth about Dr. Lori Sullivan. She sent Jess a USB containing a list of patients who suffered side effects of a narcotic street drug—Luminous."

A pause.

"We can't ask her ourselves because the woman died just days after mailing the USB... Yes, I suspect foul play... Thank you." Reece disconnected the call and put his phone back in his pocket.

"If Lori knew she was in trouble, why cryptically mail the USB? Why didn't she just call me?" Jess asked.

"Perhaps she didn't get the chance."

Jess arched an eyebrow. "They call it 'snail mail' for a reason."

He dipped his head. "Or maybe she didn't want the bad guys to know she was involving you. Instead of contacting you directly, she used old-fashioned, untraceable *snail mail*."

Jess ran a shaky hand through her hair, dragging her fingernails along her scalp.

Lori, Lori, Lori. What did you get yourself into?

MICA CHECKED her email while her son Allen took his afternoon nap. He still existed in the mostly-eat-and-sleep baby phase, but at least he was sleeping through the night and she could get some work done from home during the day. When her husband, David, wasn't working in the ER, she would go into the office for a few hours during the day, but today she was home with Allen.

She sat down in front of her laptop, scanning job requests and resumes. Since she'd hired two new employees simultaneously when she took on the Alonso twins, all jobs were currently well-covered. Yet she always checked applications for any diamonds hidden in the rough.

Claire had updated her about Reece's girlfriend—or whatever

they currently were after being forced back together. The computer guru had initially scoured Jessica Ong's flash drives, until they learned the high commodity one was still in Jess's possession. Now, Claire was combing through Dr. Lori Sullivan's internet trail of electronic data from her work email to her personal email to her social media sites.

Few secrets were safe from Claire Maltisse's bloodhound abilities. Hopefully she would find a connection between Dr. Sullivan and Fernandez that would explain his desire to pursue this USB drive of patient information.

Then what?

Mica couldn't face off against Lautaro Fernandez. Rider SI was out manned and out financed by a drug lord of his caliber. Yet, the team had taken down Titan Enterprises—an independent company known for its ruthless leader and illegal activity. Maxine Rider had orchestrated an elaborate scheme, which had culminated in the imprisonment of Lucius Titan. But the ordeal had taken inside information and endangered everyone on the team. High risk and high reward. Not the type of conflict Mica could or would engage her team in lightly.

A new email alert flickered on Mica's screen. At the sight of the sender, Mica practically growled. She read through the message twice as her stomach twisted in knots.

Slipping in her Bluetooth earbuds, she called Claire.

"I don't have any updates, Mica. Still hacking." Claire's voice had an edge to it.

Mica knew the woman had been up all night and was working extremely hard knowing someone Reece cared about was in danger.

Mica kept her voice low even though Allen slept in another room. "I know, and that's fine. Don't forget to take some breaks. This is time sensitive, but Jess is safe with Reece for now."

"Yeah, that must be awk-ward," Claire singsonged the last word.

Mica would in no way entangle herself in Reece's love life. According to the grapevine—Jess to Jenna to Claire to Mica—Reece had been the one to end things when Jess invited him to meet her parents. His fate was in his own hands. He might have rushed to save her from Lautaro's men, but those actions represented the type of man he was and didn't necessarily indicate he wanted to mend their relationship.

"I received another email from Hoyle," Mica told Claire.

Claire hesitated. "Does Lucius want to meet again?"

Hoyle was Lucius Titan's redheaded Viking of a man and his right hand. While Lucius remained safely in the state penitentiary, he communicated to the outside world through Hoyle.

Mica had invited danger when she'd visited Lucius to garner information on her last case. She knew those meetings had been only the beginning of an entanglement she really didn't want. But since Lucius was a wealth of criminal information, he was a necessary evil in her life right now.

"Hoyle's email suggests Lucius has information about Lautaro Fernandez."

"Wait. What? How does he know we're investigating the Argentinian?" Claire asked.

"News travels fast in the underworld," Mica said bitterly.

"So... he's baiting you."

Mica sighed. "Probably. Before I decide if I'm going to visit him, can you confirm through your channels that Lucius has had interactions with Lautaro? Something regular or recent?" She knew they'd had dealings years ago on at least one occasion.

"Yes, absolutely. Hold on a sec."

"Hello?" a male voice joined the call.

"Drake," Claire began, "Mica's on the line. She needs to know if Lucius had any dealings with Lautaro Fernandez that you're aware of from your time with Titan Enterprises."

Claire's husband, Drake, had worked for Lucius Titan briefly. Mica had met him after he'd rescued Claire from Lucius's men and had come to know Drake better as he worked with the Rider team. He'd been Maxine's last hire before her retirement.

"Yeah, sure did," Drake said. "He was one of the suppliers Lucius used when Lucius's high-profile clients wanted illegal drugs. Well, cocaine anyway. Heroin came from an Asian supplier."

Sh... Sugar, Mica silently pseudo-swore. The knot in her stomach tightened. "I guess I'll be visiting the scumbag to see if he has information on Lautaro to help unravel the mystery of Dr. Sullivan's involvement. Maybe it will help disentangle Dr. Ong from all of this."

"Be careful, Mica," Drake warned.

6

———————

*H*iking helped clear Jess's mind.

Reece had insisted she bundle up and take a walk to distract her from her current predicament. She kept pace behind him on the narrow trail. Because of his long legs, she had to take two steps for every one of his in order to keep up, but she was grateful for the brisk exercise keeping her warm against the early December chill in the Georgia mountains. If she had her matching purple cashmere sweater and scarf combo, she might be warmer, but she hadn't thought to pack those in her hurry to escape. She'd zipped her coat up tight but still couldn't shake the chill that had begun when she'd found Lori's flash drive.

Around her, bare tree branches of oak and maple blurred with the green needles of pine and spruce trees. Decaying leaves, having long lost their autumn luster, littered the ground.

Jess's mind clawed for information to make sense of her predicament. A dead colleague. A USB drive of patient data. A drug dealer searching for the drive as if it was the Holy Grail.

Why would Lautaro care about patient information? Maybe he

didn't, and he had only been contracted to find the drive and deliver it to someone. But who would hire a drug dealer to steal data? Did Lautaro have a side business of theft for hire? What was the missing link?

"You're unusually quiet back there," Reece said.

"I have to save my breath if I'm going to keep up with you."

He slowed his pace but said nothing.

She regretted the retort. She didn't need to drive a wedge in the already gargantuan gorge separating them. He was selflessly helping her.

"I'm trying to understand the connection between Lori Sullivan's death, the data, and the drug dealer," she said.

"It is a mystery. Perhaps the answer is in the data set."

"The patient information? By the looks of it, they're all people who suffered lung injury after an illegal drug."

"Something on there is worth killing for. We can get it to Claire and see what she can uncover."

The path widened, and they walked side by side.

"No." Jess shook her head. "That's protected patient information. I can't release that to Claire."

"I thought you said the ID number protected patients. There's no name, no social security number."

"It's *less* identifiable, but I still made a vow to guard patients' healthcare information."

"Are you certain you want to allow your ethical obligations to interfere with your safety?"

"No releasing patient data," she said with finality. "Besides, I'm the one who should comb through it. Not only am I authorized by our Institutional Review Board, but I'm the most qualified to make the connection. But the data set alone doesn't hold the answers. I need to look at each patient's full hospital chart. Since I also work at Lori's hospital in Chicago, I can pull up individual charts and see what I can find."

"You'll need an internet connection—and not the weak one currently disabled at the cabin," Reece said.

"And time. That's a mound of chart review work—when I don't even know what I'm looking for. It'll be like looking for an eosinophil in a drop of blood."

He grinned with an arched eyebrow. "Difficult, I gather?"

"Yeah. Eosinophils make up a very low percentage of the total cells in blood. What would be the Ranger analogy? Like looking for a Taliban insurgent in the Zabul province."

He grinned. "I prefer like finding an honest man in Congress."

"Fur on a rattle snake," she added brightly.

"A polar bear in a snowstorm."

"Teeth on a hen."

He laughed, that familiar, deep, silky sound wrapping her in the warmth of a rainbow. For a blissful moment, it was just the two of them hiking in the woods as they'd done on other weekend getaways.

He'd tried to convince her to join him camping a few times, but no way was she agreeing to a tent and sleeping on the floor. She would hike ten miles if he wanted to, but she would sleep in a comfortable bed after a hot shower at the end of the day. After several failed attempts to convince her to rough it, he had managed to take her glamping—glamorous camping—in a nice, rented camper.

She paused a moment and looked around the woods. "This place is serenely quiet. A walk was a good idea."

"It reminds me of the time we went to Helen. We stayed at the Valhalla Resort Hotel and hiked Raven Cliff Falls."

She warmed at the memory of long conversations on the rooftop bar, intimate dinners for two, and poolside daiquiris—

virgin for her. She smiled until she was reminded how their memory-making days had ended.

Reece had put an end to them.

She pivoted and resumed walking on the trail, taking the lead from Reece.

Her cheeks burned. He shouldn't be allowed to make her relive happy memories involving him and cause her to feel the weight of what she'd lost all over again. Surely that violated some post-breakup social etiquette code.

They finished the full three-mile loop of the trail, which brought them back to the cabin. As Jess pulled off her jacket in the entry room, Reece checked his phone.

"When do I get my phone back?" She felt ready to talk to Jenna, who could help her decompress.

He frowned even as he pulled it out of his pocket and handed it to her. "Make it brief."

When she turned on the phone, she saw that she had four voice-mail messages and seven texts from her mother.

"What's wrong?" he asked.

"It's my mother. I should call her back, but I don't know if I can keep it brief."

He traded phones with her and powered hers back off. "This one is secure. Don't mention where you are." He held eye contact a beat longer for emphasis, though his words weren't unkind.

Jess swallowed. Was he worried someone might have tapped her mother's cell phone? Or cloned it or whatever? Could her family be put in danger because of the cascade of events Lori Sullivan started? Such resentment wasn't fair to Lori. She'd been a good clinician and an excellent researcher who'd clearly discovered something she shouldn't have.

Something which had gotten her killed. Jess was sure of it.

Reece was still standing with the phone extended to her, watching her expression as though trying to read her thoughts.

She took it and murmured, "Thank you."

She dialed her mother's number.

"Hello?"

"Hi, Mom."

"Jessica," she snapped. "Why are you calling from a blocked number? Why didn't you call me sooner? Did you get the dumplings?"

The dumplings. Of course her mother would call her four times over dumplings. Her mother gave her gifts, but the unspoken stipulation was that Jess must call immediately and express gratitude. Waiting until the next time they spoke—which was usually twice per week—was entirely too long.

Gifts with strings attached.

Her mother needed immediate acknowledgment. Without it, Jess would be made to feel ungrateful, and on came the guilt trip.

She remembered the slip in her mailbox indicating she had a package too large for her box. "I got the dumplings, Mom. Thank you. I just finished a stretch of nights."

"You didn't call me. I raised only polite daughters."

Jess refrained from mentioning the robbers as an excuse for not calling, especially as she didn't think it would defuse the situation. "Mom—"

"You don't love me anymore?" The brisk question was all too familiar.

Jess glanced at Reece, who probably could hear her mom's loud voice through the phone. He gave an amused quirk of his lips before turning and busying himself making tea.

"Of course, I love you. How's Pops?" She paced the living room as she talked.

"You haven't visited us."

"I was in Chicago last month," she protested. She had visited at Thanksgiving, and it had been so cold that Jess wondered why she didn't move to Atlanta permanently. She glanced at Reece—there was one good reason.

Her mom protested, "You left us for some boy. And when he left you, you didn't come back."

"Mom—" Jess deflated into the chair at the kitchen table. "I like my job in Atlanta."

"Thirty-six and my daughter's not married."

"Can we *not* discuss this right now?" Jess rubbed her temple.

She wasn't prepared for the same defensive argument—why wasn't being a successful career woman enough? She also liked living in Atlanta near her friend Jenna.

"Li is a good boy. Why'd you dump him?"

"We had one date. And he was running a tech scamming company." *And that was three years ago,* Jess wanted to scream. The woman let nothing go. On that thought, she glanced at Reece who'd accused her of the same thing on more than one occasion. Maybe he was right.

Her mother gave a disgusted noise of disagreement.

"Look, Mom, I need to go."

"Cats. Your father and I will buy you cats. No more dumplings."

Jess pinched the bridge of her nose. "Thanks for implying I'll grow old and stay single."

"What about that boy Chou?"

"Bye, Mom. Love you. I'll call you in a few days."

Jess disconnected the call with her mother as Reece set a cup of tea on the table in front of her. He placed it so the handle was perfectly positioned for her to grasp.

"Thank you." She handed his phone back and took a sip of tea.

As the liquid warmed her core, she imagined Reece sensing

her distress and pulling her into his arms. She wanted human contact and a hug—to feel the power of his long, powerful arms and absorb his strength. But she couldn't ask for such a thing and risk appearing weak.

"You okay?" Reece asked.

"Yeah." She glanced at the laptop. "Can I make one more call?"

He nodded, handing the phone back to her.

Jess called her brother, willing herself to keep her composure for the discussion. She needed to hear a friendly voice.

"Hello?"

"Hi, Jay. I just finished talking to Mom. How's the family?"

"Great. Everyone's good. We had a playdate. A dozen girls making gingerbread houses. Now everyone is cracked out on sugar."

Jess could picture hyper ten-year-olds destroying Jay's living room like kittens wild on catnip. "You want me to call back at a better time?"

"No, no. Your timing is good. You're my excuse to step into the other room and take a breather. How is work?"

"The usual winter ICU overflow with viral infections and heart failure. I'm off for a couple of days though."

"Mom called me wondering if you'd make it to Christmas."

Jess chuckled. "I missed one year because I had to work a shift, and she worries every time since. I will be there, although I should threaten not to come because she keeps wanting to set me up with a man. Who sets up blind dates for their daughter on Christmas?"

"She would pick other calendar dates, but you're in Atlanta half the time."

Jess caught the slight jab in his tone.

"I like Atlanta—the weather, the job, the friends."

"Sure, we just thought you'd come back when things didn't work out with Peanut Butter Cup."

Jay had begun calling Reece that ever since Jess first told him about their rocky relationship. He'd said the nickname fit, not only because of his given name, but because the relationship seemed to be sticky like peanut butter. The only thing Jay's comparison did for Jess was remind her that Reece was good enough to eat and as addictive as a rich chocolate-peanut butter combination loaded with sugar.

"I moved for many reasons, and those other reasons are still applicable," she said.

"So PBC is out of your life for good?"

Oh, boy. She avoided looking in Reece's direction. He had walked to the fireplace where he poked at the woodpile.

"No. Maybe. I don't know. The situation has become more complicated."

"He can't commit, Jess. That's not complicated. That's spineless." Jay sighed when she didn't respond. "Live where you want to live. I just want you to be happy. I'm not sure this guy makes you happy. I have to go. I'll see you at Christmas?"

"Yeah, see you then." She listened to the phone disconnect and the ensuing silence as she digested Jay's words.

She had her own perceptions about happiness. She was responsible for her happiness—no one else. Happiness was a state of mind she either chose to be in or not. What she sought in Reece was companionship and fulfilment. If she couldn't have those things, she was the one who would decide if she would be happy about it or not.

But she understood Jay's point—she wanted a long-term relationship with a man who didn't want the same things, or at least not to the depth to which she wanted.

She raised her cup of tea and took a sip. "I need to work," she told Reece. "Where are we going for internet access?"

"My place."

She choked. "Like hell."

Reece's eye twitched, but Jess didn't care if she pissed him off. She had no intention of spending five minutes in his house with all of their memories peppering her into sensory overload.

"Jess—"

"We'll go to the Rider headquarters," she said. "It's secure, right? Jenna told me Claire holed up there for weeks when Lucius was after her."

Reece had explained his reasoning for distancing himself from Jess during that dangerous time while the Rider team was dealing with Titan Enterprises and Lucius Titan who had systematically tried to eliminate each Rider employee.

Reece crossed his arms as he walked from the fireplace toward her. "Rider HQ is situated too close to downtown Atlanta. I'm not sitting in traffic with you for two hours to get there."

She leaned back in her chair. "There must be some other place."

"My place is remote with a state-of-the-art security system and firepower. There's no other place closer and safer."

She felt her breath come in ragged heaves. Did he know what he was asking of her? Did he comprehend the wounds he would open by taking her back there? But she didn't want to let him see her pain. She wouldn't show weakness.

She pushed away from the table and left the room.

"Where are you going?" he called after her.

"To pack. The sooner we get there, the sooner I can get to the bottom of this."

And the sooner her heartache could transform from a sharp, clawing pain back to a dull ache.

7

———

Reece watched Jess go down the hall toward her room and swore under his breath. The vehemence with which she initially refused going to his place had knifed him.

Did she hate him so much that she couldn't spend a few days in his space? But something else lurked beneath her anger—pain. Pain he'd caused and that evidently still hovered under the rippling surface like a vicious crocodile waiting to snap.

He didn't know how to repair the damage he'd done, but he did want to try. He had wanted to fix it for months now but hadn't known how. He'd assumed Jess wanted nothing more to do with him, but her recent behavior suggested her feelings were still raw. And raw emotions meant she still gave a damn about him.

Bringing her to his house wasn't a ploy to get closer to her. The location was the safest place to venture to on short notice, aside from the cabin where they already were. The cabin had the advantage of being completely off radar—under none of the Rider's team names. The downside was the lack of sufficient internet bandwidth.

He texted Santino and asked him to check on his house and verify it was safe.

Will do, came the immediate reply.

Reece's place ran the risk of someone looking there if they learned of Jess's relationship with him. But while she had photos of them together and had posted on social media, she had followed his request to never put his name in the taglines. He'd insisted on that rule while dating because of his occasional under-cover work for Rider SI and the need for discretion.

She'd asked him once if he felt embarrassed to be seen with her. Hell no—he was the one who felt like a second-class citizen beside her glamour and glitz, like Angelina Jolie and Billy Bob Thornton. Why wasn't she embarrassed to be seen with him?

Reece recalled the time he'd ended a vacation getaway early because he'd needed to join a case with Ryan. Weapons developer and Rider client Bill Sharp had asked specifically for them to be on the protection detail for a prototype demonstration since the pair of them had been the ones to save Sharp's billion-dollar drone collection on a previous assignment.

They'd finished the detail, which transpired without a hiccup, and had gone out for drinks afterward, just the two of them.

Reece had checked his watch. "Jess ought to be flying back now."

"I'm sorry you got pulled away from vacation." Ryan drank his beer. "Usually we have more advanced notice for these things."

"I know the Sharp account is important to Maxine." He swirled the glass of whisky, watching the smooth bronze liquid flow around the ice cubes.

"Still, it was your first international vacation together."

"At least I only missed the last two days."

"How was the rest of the trip?" Ryan asked.

"I hear in your tone, Walsh, that you're longing to know about a deeper connection. Unlike you, I'm not a romantic sap. We had a lovely time. I'll say no more."

"If you had a nice time, and you're not mad about the mission pulling you away, why do you look like the thundercloud after someone stole your sunshine?"

"It's juvenile."

Ryan shrugged. "Issues of the heart often can be."

"Jess wasn't upset."

"What do mean?"

"I told Jess I had to leave for a mission, and she didn't complain. She didn't ask me to stay. I didn't think she would cry or whine, but I did expect a little incredulity that I would be called away to work."

"Sounds to me like she respects your priorities."

Reece sipped his drink. "I thought she would give me some type of pushback. Instead, she accepted the news and said she would stay and finish the trip without me. Not an ounce of bitterness or bite in her voice."

Ryan arched an eyebrow. "You're upset she didn't fight with you *for you*." He chuckled.

"I told you my reaction was juvenile." Reece took a sip of his whiskey.

"You wanted her to pout and sulk and tell you the paradise vacation wouldn't be the same without you. But she turned lemons into lemonade." Ryan smacked a hand against Reece's shoulder. "Don't take it personally. She works hard and probably needed the vacation with or without you. You're not afraid she'll hook up with the cabana boy?"

"No, nothing like that. I just... well, I think back to all the times I laughed at the schmucks who found comfort in their women pining away with worry in the States while they risked their lives overseas. I never wanted that. I've never been like those men. So, when Jess said, 'Stay safe, see you when the mission is over,' as if I was making a trip down the road for takeout, my initial reaction was to wonder if she gave a damn about me. Then, I was disgusted with myself for wanting her to show a little more troubled emotion, especially when I didn't show her any myself."

Ryan took another swig of his beer. "You want to be wanted. That's human. Did you tell her you would miss her?"

"No."

"Maybe if you had, she would've reciprocated, and you would feel better about knowing she has feelings for you. You could always text her now..." Ryan's voice trailed off.

Reece knew he'd never been good at showing his vulnerability first—being the one to lower his guard first.

But if he was serious about a relationship with Jess, that would have to change.

MICA GAVE David a peck on the cheek when he arrived home a little after six thirty.

He dropped his keys on the counter. "Smells fantastic in here."

"I cooked." She smiled, taking a lingering look at his disheveled brown hair and warm eyes.

"I know. That's twice in one week. I could get used to this working-from-home thing. How's Allen?"

"Blissfully sleeping. I wore him out with tummy time." She liked her time at home but always felt she got more accomplished when she was physically at the office. She was learning that the life of a mother meant a constant tug-of-war between home life and work life.

David wrapped her in a hug from behind as she stirred the chili.

"How was your day?" he asked.

Mica considered how to answer David's question as she relaxed in his embrace.

"That bad, huh? How about I fix you a drink?"

Mica rolled her shoulders. "That sounds nice."

As her husband set to work making a decaf coffee with Baily's Irish Cream, she glanced at him with adoration—she was so fortunate to have found a man who supported her career and was turning out to be a phenomenal father.

"Do you remember Jessica Ong?" Mica asked.

"Yeah, Jenna's friend, and she works in the ICU. She has family in Chicago, so she splits her time between here and there."

"She had a break-in yesterday at her apartment."

"Oh, no." He placed the cup of spiked coffee in front of Mica as she leaned on the counter.

"She's okay. Reece was pretty quick to spring into action."

"Are they still dating?"

"I'm told he has commitment issues."

"They're a bit like oil and water, aren't they?" David said with an amused grin. "But the times when we've gathered for Rider SI functions, I thought they looked good together. They're both good people. Staff and patients have nothing but good things to say about Jess and her bedside manner. And didn't Reece have some outstanding performance with the Rangers?"

"Yeah, he earned a commendation medal. I can only speculate that his relationship commitment issues stem from either the things he's seen or the things he's done."

"So, if Jess is okay, what has you wound a little tight?"

Mica took another sip of her coffee and ran a hand through her short blonde hair. "The thieves were looking for something specific, a USB drive. Since they are now in police custody, and the man who hired them doesn't have what he was after, Jess may still be in danger."

"Good thing she has the Rider team looking after her."

"Yes." Mica granted him a smile. "For now, she's safe with Reece, and we're looking into how best to help her."

"So, nothing to do this evening but unwind and tackle everything fresh tomorrow."

"Hmm. Yes."

His voice dropped to a husky whisperer as he tugged her by the apron into his arms. "Which means I can help you relax and unwind as we seize this opportunity while Allen is sleeping."

She reached over and cut the flame off from under the pot of chili. "I think that's an excellent idea."

Tonight, she could enjoy her family and forget about drug dealers and violence and kidnappings for a little while.

***

JESS RODE in the passenger seat of her car with her chair fully reclined as she stared up at the starlit sky through the sunroof. They'd stopped at a car charging station to "fill-up" the Tesla before Reece drove them to his house.

She thought about when she first met Reece at Jenna's wedding. Jenna and Ryan had a destination wedding in Antigua on the property Jenna's parents owned. The day had been picture-perfect—crystal clear water in sparkling teal and emerald beneath a sky of the purest blue. Jess had been ecstatic for her friend's happiness, and appropriately jealous in her role as the best friend who was still single.

Reece had been the best man—complete with a dashing tuxedo. The cowboy boots he'd worn had caught Jess's eye. He was over a foot taller than her with a lean figure that moved effortlessly. His facial features were ruggedly handsome with keen eyes she would later learn turned dark and smoky during moments of intimacy.

His mustache had intrigued her because she never cared much for facial hair. However, Reece's calm demeanor, combined with the humorous twinkle in his eye like he knew a secret you didn't, and cowboy boots, enabled him to pull off the look. Even when he was angry, the mustache added effect. It seemed to grow straighter when he was annoyed and puffed out just a little when he was infuriated—almost as if the decoration could match Reece's emotions the way a mood ring changed color.

After the wedding ceremony, he had asked her to dance. Since pickings were slim at a Caribbean destination wedding, she'd initially suspected he was just trying to pass the time for the evening rather than having a genuine interest in her—unless he was an opposites-attract kind of guy. Since he was cute and she wanted to dance in her new dress and heels, she had accepted.

"Jenna told me you work in security like Ryan." She had started the conversation.

"Precisely. And Ryan told me you work in the ICU like Jenna."

"That's right. We did our residency and fellowship together," Jess said.

"I'm not acquainted with the healthcare field. You'll have to educate me on those terms."

"Residency is the training that follows medical school. Fellowship is the training that follows residency. So, I did four years of medical school, followed by three years of internal medicine residency, followed by two years of critical care fellowship."

His lips turned into an appreciative grin. "That sounds immensely laborious. I'm impressed, though knowing you carry the title of MD is impressive in and of itself."

"I happen to find the title of Army Ranger impressive. How long did you serve?"

"Ten years. Afghanistan. Iraq. Syria."

"You must have traveled extensively between being an Army Ranger and your current job. Jenna told me Ryan had been to Moscow before they traveled there together."

"I've been to most major Asian and European countries with my private security work."

She noted how well they danced together, not missing a step. He made smaller steps seemingly effortlessly to accommodate her short stature.

"London?" she asked.

"Yes."

"Paris?"

"Yes."

"Rotterdam?"

"Amsterdam."

"I did a European trip one summer during medical school—London, Paris, and Rotterdam," she said.

"Did you take the train from London to France?" he asked.

"I did."

"Did you mind the gap?" He grinned.

She chuckled. "I certainly did."

"Little thing like you could fall through the gap and never be heard from again." He twirled her in a circle.

"I'm fairly outspoken. No one has ever been worried they would never hear from me again."

He laughed, his eyes twinkling. "What was your favorite part of your travels?"

"Shopping, of course. The museums were nice too. But definitely the shopping."

He shook his head with a chuckle.

"Shopping is funny?" she asked, amused by his amusement.

"You seem exceedingly well put together, Dr. Ong, and I couldn't help but think of the book-turned-movie *Crazy Rich Asians* the minute I saw you. So, yes, it's humorous that your shopping interests corroborate my stereotype."

"I'm not sure if that's an insult or a compliment, Ranger Owen, but all I'm choosing to hear is that I'm exceedingly well put together."

"And beautiful."

"Now you're just buttering me up."

"Can you blame me? It's a wedding on a tropical island. Magic is in the air."

This time, she laughed. "Do you believe in magic, Reece?" She would find it hard for a Ranger and a man of his practicality to believe in magic. And if he tried to give her some nonsense about love at first sight, she'd laugh in his face. He was obviously a player, and nobody played Jess.

"I believe in the laws of attraction. You're an attractive woman. We're on a Caribbean island. The night is our oyster."

When the song stopped, he took a step back. "Can I get you a glass of champagne?"

"I don't drink."

He frowned.

"Asian genes." She shrugged. If her inability to drink turned him off, he could walk away. "I have a deficiency of aldehyde dehydrogenase. Can't break down alcohol."

He cocked his head to one side. "I'm fascinated. What happens when you drink?"

"With as little as a thimbleful, I get facial flushing."

"Might be fun to watch."

"I'm not a show pony." She also generally felt like crap if she took even a sip.

His smiled faded as he gave a slight bow of his head. "My apologies. My intrigue wasn't meant to offend."

"Do you always talk so... eloquently?"

"No. Sometimes I curse. Sometimes my loquaciousness drives others to curse."

She snickered. "We made it through an entire dance, and neither of us have cursed yet."

"Then let's have another." He swept her back onto the dance floor.

She adored his charm, and when she went back to his room for the night, she understood he was a man who didn't form attachments to women. She accepted that and was content to indulge in a one-night stand. While such activity was a rare occurrence for her, she'd been aroused enough by his charm to find the idea intriguing.

She hadn't expected the sex to be so amazing, but he'd taken her to the next level. She suspected he'd enjoyed the delicious intimacy as much as she had, but she didn't stick around to have a conversation about it. In the early morning, she did as etiquette dictated for a one-night stand—she left. And she had the pleasure of reliving the night in her imagination over and over without the expectation of ever hearing from him again.

8

───────

*B*y the time they arrived at Reece's house—a single-story three-bedroom home on ten acres just north of Alpharetta—a large moon loomed over them.

Reece eased Jess's car slowly down the paved drive, remembering the first time he'd brought Jess here and the way she'd complimented the landscape—maples arching over the drive and a weeping willow behind a three-tiered stone fountain in the front yard of the house. All was barren this time of year, but spring and summer were lush and beautiful, and fall was splashes of vibrant autumn colors.

The drive made a loop in front of his house, but a tail of asphalt also continued another fifty feet to dead end into the garage beside the house.

He recalled the times she'd complained that the drive from her apartment to his place took an hour. He'd taken that to mean she wanted him to invite her to live with him, but Reece hadn't been ready for that level of commitment. Maybe if he hadn't been so shortsighted, their relationship would look very different right now.

His gaze slid to Jess dozing in the passenger seat. He would have liked to joke that he'd worn her out arguing about where they would stay—Rider SI versus his place—but she was probably more exhausted from the stress of everything revolving around the flash drive.

When he parked outside the garage, Santino stood there, leaning on his champagne-colored Pontiac Grand Am on the drive loop. The house lights were on, indicating his partner had swept the premises as Reece had requested.

He exited the car and shook hands with Santino. "Thanks, man."

"All secure," Santino said. "How's Sleeping Beauty?"

"Frazzled. But she deals with crises for a living, so she's keeping her wits about her."

"Crazy nice car. First time I saw her Tesla at the cabin, my jaw dropped."

"She works her ass off and rewards herself accordingly." Reece smiled as he used Jess's own words and found himself agreeing with her.

"What now?"

"Tomorrow she'll log onto the hospital server and do some sleuthing."

"And you?"

"I'm going to hit the streets and do a different type of sleuthing." He absolutely couldn't be idle in his own house with his ex-girlfriend occupying the same space. She would probably appreciate him making himself scarce so her anger toward him would be less of a distraction.

Santino opened his car door. "Call me when you're on the move, and I'll join you. I suspect your *sleuthing* involves finding some of Lautaro's men, in which case you may need backup. *Alguien a cubre tu trasero.*"

Reece shifted his weight on his feet. "Actually, I was hoping to impose upon you to watch over Jess while I run my errands."

Santino frowned. "You want me to babysit your girlfriend?"

"Firstly, not my girlfriend. And hardly a baby. Secondly, you'll be protecting a Rider SI client. She specifically asked to hire our services." He knew Mica would never bill Jess, but he spoke the truth about Jess's offer.

Santino ran a hand through his chocolate-brown hair. "Yeah. Sure. I'll look after her."

"Back at eight a.m."

"Back at eight." Santino climbed in his car and drove away from Reece's house.

Reece turned back to the Tesla. Typical Jess—still asleep. And she was the epitome of a Sleeping Beauty with dark hair and pale skin. So peaceful—unlike the times when she was awake and lashing out at him. Admittedly, he often enjoyed her appearance then too—all heat and animated irritation that had her cheeks flushing and eyes flashing. He opened the passenger side door and looked down at her curled in a ball.

"Come on, darling. You can't sleep in the car—even though it costs as much as a small townhouse." He bent and scooped her into his arms.

She helped by hooking her arms around his neck. His chest fluttered at their proximity and her embrace. He tempered the warmth spreading through his body. He didn't need to read too much into her acceptance of him carrying her.

After climbing the porch steps, he bent while holding Jess to enter the key code to unlock the front door, part of his state-of-the-art home security system.

He carried her over the threshold and into the guest bedroom where he gently he laid her on the bed. "I'll bring your things inside."

"Can you stay close?" Her voice sounded small and hollow—as if she'd been drained from the inside out. The vulnerability tugged at his heart.

"Let me grab your bags, lock the house, and I'll be right back."

"Okay."

He finished all of those things and returned to her room. Since she'd fallen back to sleep, he took the opportunity to shower. To avoid the temptation to pursue anything sexual while she was emotionally vulnerable, he returned to her room fully dressed in blue jeans and a T-shirt and lay above the covers. At least she would see he'd stayed close, as promised, all night.

JESS WOKE the next morning beside a sleeping Reece. She resisted the urge to roll over into his arms—or roll completely on top of him. She knew all too well how sublime he felt pressed against her.

Instead, she quietly escaped, rolling out of bed. She grabbed her toiletry bag and clean clothes and headed to the bathroom.

When she emerged, the bedroom was empty.

In the living room, she found Santino sitting on the couch, reading *América Economía*. He lowered his magazine and turned to look at her. She'd met him once before at an office function—somebody's birthday perhaps. He had dark skin and bright teeth set in a strong jaw. His mahogany hair was trimmed short.

"Good morning, Dr. Ong." His accent held just a hint of South American undertones.

"Please, it's just Jess. How are you, Santino?"

"The sun is shining, and life is good." He smiled. "*El sol brilla para todos.*"

She heated a cup of tea in the microwave. "The sun does shine for everyone, but sometimes you feel cold anyway. He's gone, isn't he?"

"Yes, *señorita.*" His tone was apologetic.

She dropped a tea bag in her cup before turning to the refrigerator. She pulled out lactose-free yogurt and fruit and made herself a parfait.

"He just left," she scoffed.

Stay close, she'd told Reece last night. She silently scolded herself as she irritably poked at the tea bag floating in her cup. That must have sounded like a damsel-in-distress ploy.

She stirred her fruit parfait. She wasn't a damsel in distress, was she? She prided herself on her independence. If she wanted something, she worked for it and earned it or she bought it for herself.

"I think he feels like he needs to do something to help," Santino said.

"By endangering himself? By going after answers and confronting drug dealers?" Her tone betrayed her worry and frustration.

He shrugged like such activities were just another day at the office. Maybe they were for people like him and Reece.

"I don't need that type of help," she said. Reece's type of help could get him killed.

"What type of help do you need?" Santino closed his magazine and turned sideways on the couch to look at her fully.

"I don't know." She stirred her tea.

"He's worried about you. He wants to do something. *Yo creo que* he never knows what you need, even before now." His tone was soft, empathetic.

She wondered if Santino's knowledge had been gained through observation or if Reece had opened up to him.

"I don't need anything from anyone except their time and companionship," she said, half pleading. "I have friends at work and online because of the enjoyment we gain from each other's company. Why do I have to *need* anything from him?"

Santino cocked his head to one side in thoughtful reflection. "A man wants a woman who needs him. What does one give an independent, self-sufficient woman if she can buy anything for herself?"

"Love," she answered simply. "We had a nice routine when our time in Atlanta or Chicago overlapped. I would come home and have tea. We would sit on the couch, and he would rub my feet as we talked about our day." Sometimes they got frisky, and other times they submerged in comfortable conversation.

"Sounds nice."

"Yeah, so nice I thought maybe we could make it more official —and until Reece, I'd never thought about making any man a permanent addition to my life."

"You proposed?" Santino's eyebrows shot up.

"No, but apparently I did the next worst thing by asking him to meet my parents."

He chuckled. "That doesn't seem so bad." He stroked his chin. "I can't defend Reece's actions. You obviously care about him, so I don't understand why he let you go. *Quizás, él es un idiota.*"

She snorted her agreement, but didn't necessarily feel any better about the situation after having earned Santino's sympathy.

"'*Por qué, si el amor es lo contrario a la guerra, es una guerra en sí?*'" he said wistfully.

"Okay. Now you've gone beyond my meager knowledge of Spanish. Something about love and war?"

Santino grinned. "'Why, if love is the opposite of war, is it a war in itself?' Written by Benito Pérez Galdós, a novelist from Spain."

"I believe that quote sums up my relationship with Reece perfectly." She shoveled a bite of parfait into her mouth and moved to sit in front of her laptop at the table. "Time to work."

She couldn't worry about her relationship with Reece or what trouble he was getting himself into right now. She needed to focus on solving the immediate problem and would tackle the rest later.

REECE DROVE his silver F-150 toward downtown Atlanta as he called a buddy of his and Rider SI's most recent satisfied client—DEA agent PJ Tuder. He'd phoned Reece five days ago when his daughter had been kidnapped. They'd rescued her just before Reece rushed off to save Jess at her apartment.

"Reece, I'm glad you called. I didn't get to thank you in person."

"You're very welcome, PJ. I hope your daughter recovers swiftly."

"Thank you. If I can ever repay you..." his voice trailed off.

"It seems my dealings with Lautaro Fernandez are only in their infancy."

"Oh. Why is that?"

"He sent his minions after a friend of mine," Reece said, trying not to allow the words to conjure images of Jess having been assaulted in her own apartment.

"He didn't waste any time retaliating. Is your friend okay? How did Fernandez know you helped me?"

"Yes, she is unharmed. And I don't believe the Argentinian does know. The events are intriguingly unrelated."

A moment of silence hung in the air where the hum of Reece's truck on the interstate was the only sound he heard.

"I guess this is the part where you reveal the reason for your call." PJ said, his voice tight as though he thought Reece might ask him to get involved again with the drug dealer the day after his daughter had been safely returned to him.

"I only need information," Reece assured him. "I need to exchange words with someone in Lautaro's organization."

"Words or blows?" PJ asked wryly.

Reece and PJ had known each other since their days as Rangers together. They knew some things couldn't be resolved diplomatically.

"That will be determined by the level of cooperation I receive from the drug dealer. I need a name and a location."

PJ sighed. "Juan Penaloza is one of Lautaro's dealers in Atlanta, but he could be at any of his clubs or apartment buildings. You're not going to be able to track him down in a timely fashion."

Reece could have pushed PJ for further contacts. Surely the man knew people in the Atlanta PD narcotics department who kept hourly tabs on the drug dealers in hopes of catching them in illegal activity. A few phone calls or in-person visits and PJ could churn information out of his contacts, unless they had a sting running and refused to relinquish details. But PJ had just gotten his daughter back after a terrifying several days, and Reece didn't want to force him back to work.

"Where do his lackeys deal?"

"Reece—"

"I'm only asking for a street corner."

"Kirkwood," PJ said reluctantly.

"Thank you." Reece was familiar with a dozen shady places in Atlanta, including Kirkwood, but he didn't know which drug dealers had laid claim to which locations.

"Try not to shoot anyone," PJ teased.

"I never draw first, you know that."

"I know that," PJ said. "I just don't want to bury any more friends this year. The war on drugs is never-ending."

Reece grimaced. He knew the stats. "What do you know about Luminous?"

"Illegal drug. Its popularity is spreading due to its highly addictive nature. Chicago to New York to Atlanta. West Coast is probably next."

"Are you laying low?" Reece asked.

"Yeah, I'm out. Shit got real when they went after my family. I want to nail Lautaro, but not at my family's expense. And I'm no use to my wife and daughter if I die in the line of duty."

Hearing the conflict in his friend's voice, Reece reassured him, "You're doing the right thing."

"And you're no use to your friend either if you get killed on this little escapade," PJ added.

"Then I'd best not get killed."

9

*J*ess weighed her options. She could curl up in a ball, mourn Lori, and feel sorry for herself. Or she could crack the code of Lori's delivery and honor her colleague's memory by uncovering the truth.

She logged into her hospital account which required her to briefly turn her phone on for two-factor remote verification. Once she had access to patient records through the electronic medical record, she turned her phone back off. She began skimming patient charts, hoping to find anything to connect the dots of Lori's spreadsheet to drug dealers.

After an hour and a half of intense focus, her vision blurred from eye fatigue as she stared at the computer screen. She closed her eyes for a moment of rest.

Even though Reece had left the house, her thoughts wandered to him.

She recalled the time he had showed up at her apartment after a rumble related to his Rider SI work. His forearms and knuckles had been bruised and battered, and he'd had a nasty gash on his arm.

"Miss me, darling?"

"What the hell, Reece?"

He'd been keeping his distance because someone wanted the entire Rider team dead, and he hadn't wanted Jess to become a target by association. Or so he'd claimed.

"Try again," he drawled. "You're too worried to sound angry."

She let him inside and ushered him to her red couch. At least he was ambulatory.

After stripping off his shirt, she assessed the damage. "Don't bleed on my couch," she warned.

"It's a red couch."

"I still don't want blood on it."

He chuckled.

"I need my first aid kit." She walked toward her bathroom.

"Got any alcohol? I could use a drink," he called after her.

She wanted to lie and say no. Since she had worried he was avoiding her rather than protecting her, she'd thought about trashing his stash of whiskey out of spite. She sure didn't drink the crap, but he liked the occasional nightcap—only ever one. If she threw the liquor away, would the action be representative of the end of their relationship? A *real* end as opposed to the many "breaks" they'd taken? Ultimately, she'd kept the whiskey just as she'd kept his toothbrush and a few changes of clothes—burning that eternal flame that they would always reunite. The flame that threatened to spontaneously combust her heart.

She returned to him on the couch with his drink on the rocks and her first aid bag. She had an enhanced kit with the usual bandages and antiseptics but also some sutures and local anesthetic which she'd stocked with him in mind.

He downed the whiskey and braced himself. "Okay. I'm ready."

She rolled her eyes. "This isn't third world medicine where I hand you a stick to bite down on. I'm going to numb the laceration with lidocaine first."

"Oh. Marvelous. I knew I'd come to the right place."

"I'm not a plastic surgeon though. Don't expect perfect stitches resulting in a perfect scar."

He grinned. "Perfect is dull and overrated."

She cleaned the wound with its jagged edges. Either someone came after him with a steak knife or a very dull blade.

"Is that why you do what you do?" she asked without making eye contact. "You work for Rider because it's not dull?"

She could feel him watching her work—drawing the lidocaine up into a syringe and numbing the skin using a small needle.

"There are many exceedingly dull hours, days, and weeks with Rider SI." He leaned back and closed his eyes, keeping his arm still as she worked. "I do this job because it's how I make a difference. We—that being the Rider team—have a unique skill set. Few can do what we do, take the risks we take. We help people— whether that's catching an embezzler or taking down a rogue security team like Titan Enterprises."

She listened quietly as she sutured, trying to comprehend his words.

"You don't believe me?" His voice held more sorrow than incredulity.

"I believe you have the ability and willingness to do what others can't or won't. I just wonder if you know the toll it takes on your body."

He leaned forward, again keeping his arm still. "Dr. Ong, you have a unique skill set. Don't you go to work every day feeling like you make a difference in peoples' lives?"

She glanced up from her sewing. "Most days." Looking back down, she tied the next knot.

He continued, "You work long shifts, finish hungry, dehydrated, and emotionally exhausted. I wonder if you know the toll it takes on your body." He tossed her own words lightly back at her.

She tied the last suture, amazed he'd never flinched through the whole process.

With his free hand, he reached up and tucked a strand of hair behind her ear. "Are we so different?"

"I take breaks, de-stress, shop, travel, pamper myself. I balance work life and home life."

He drank the remnants of whiskey and melted ice from his glass before setting it back down and leaning back against the couch once more. "Spending time with you is my balance."

His words touched her deeply. She tried to still her fluttering heart as she wrapped the bandage around the stitched wound. By the time she'd finished and composed her thoughts to tell him how romantic his words were, he'd fallen fast asleep on her couch.

REECE CRUISED the Kirkwood area until he spotted a suitable mark. He parked a block away on La France Street.

When he got out of his truck, he pulled on his bullet-resistant blazer—a three-thousand-dollar perk of working for a security company. He holstered the backup weapon from his glove compartment into his waist for easy access. He buttoned the blazer but purposefully left the gun exposed, wanting to convey to his victim that he meant business. From the storage compartment in the bed of his truck, he withdrew a stiff lariat and tossed it over his shoulder.

He approached a shifty, pale-faced kid, probably not a day over twenty-years old. The dealer scanned the streets even as he tried to look casual, leaning against a brick wall with his hands stuffed in his baggy black jeans. When he noticed Reece, a wary look entered his eyes as though he was trying to decide if Reece was a threat or a buyer.

As Reece walked closer—fifty feet away now—the kid's body language favored a flight response with tense muscles ready to push off the wall and sprint.

And so he did.

Reece dropped the bulk of the rope into his left hand and spun the other end with his right. When he had the rhythm, he let the rope loose. It dropped over the sprinter's head and around his torso.

Reece planted his feet as he tugged. The lariat cinched tight, pinning the kid's arms to his sides and bringing him to a violent halt. He landed with a howl on his backside in the alley.

Reece strolled toward him, recoiling the rope along the way.

"Police brutality!" the kid cried.

"It would be, except I'm not the police," Reece said.

The kid reached into a pocket and pulled out a switchblade. He was hardly a threat on his back with his hands plastered to his sides, but he might cut the rope.

Reece kicked the knife out of his hand. "I only want to talk."

"Screw you. You piece of shit cowboy."

"I'm going to bend down and frisk your pockets."

The kid spit toward Reece, and the glob landed on the asphalt at his feet.

"It seems we aren't going to achieve this on civilized terms."

The kid cursed at him again.

In a fluid move, Reece bent, flipped the kid onto his stomach, and tied his thrashing legs together with the rope.

When he checked his pockets, he found a keyring and little bags containing five to ten small white pills.

"Is this the new drug? Luminous?" He shook a packet in the kid's face.

"Get that thing out of my face, asshole!" He tagged on a few more colorful expletives.

"How about Juan Penaloza? Do you know where he is right now?"

"Who wants to know? Your mother?"

Reece dragged him around behind a dumpster as the kid continued to swear. The area wasn't crowded, but the kid's wailing would draw unwanted attention.

"Wait. Wait. Don't kill me." He'd apparently drawn the wrong conclusion about Reece moving his body.

Reece waved the packet of pills in the air.

"Yeah. Yeah. That's Luminous."

"And Juan?"

"Z Club. He does his books in the back office this time of day." The kid added a bitter chuckle.

Reece tucked the drug sample inside his jacket. "Something's funny?"

"If you go in there, it's your funeral, man."

Reece continued to check the kid's pockets and found his mobile phone. After holding it in front of the kid's face and unlocking it using the facial recognition software, Reece changed the settings to passcode rather than facial recognition. Then, he reset the passcode.

"What are you doing?" the kid asked.

"Picking out carnations for my funeral." Reece pocketed the phone.

He looked back down at the kid with a frown. He hated to lose his lariat, but Reece couldn't let the kid free and risk him ruining his plans.

"Hey! Where are you going? You can't leave me here like this."

Reece walked away. "I'd untie you, but you're going to attempt to spit on me again."

"No. I won't. Untie me!"

Reece raised his hands. "You have failed to establish any trust with your juvenile behavior." He turned the corner and walked back to his car.

He typed "Z Club" into his phone map application and drove his truck to East Atlanta Village. Once there, he circled the block in his vehicle. The establishment was closed, as it was only noon. The whitewashed cinder block building had a rectangular shape. The neon sign, currently not glowing, had a logo with an outline of a naked woman relaxing in a martini glass beside the name "Z Club." Around back sat a black Lincoln Continental with tinted windows and a man leaning against it engrossed in his mobile phone.

Reece parked two blocks away and withdrew the phone he'd stolen from the street dealer. He scrolled through texts messages and chat apps, getting a sense of who the kid's friends were, who were fellow drug dealers, and who were superiors. The syntax and slang changed based on who the kid had electronically interacted with in the various modalities.

Reece typed a fake text message: *Pigs almost busted me on the street. Overheard talk of a raid at Z's.*

He copied and pasted the message into multiple text message streams that seemed work-related and lastly into a social app with people who'd been chatting about vague "deliveries" and "hot spots"—who most certainly weren't referring to pizza and wireless internet.

Reece would wait to press send on everything.

With his plan set, he exited his truck and moved into position.

Jess read through histories, admissions, discharge summaries, laboratory results, and imaging reports as she made notes directly into the spreadsheet Lori had sent her while also scribbling on a sketch pad she'd found in Reece's library.

Yes, the man had a library. She loved his house, with the enormous master bathroom and walk-in closet, the library complete with rolling wall ladder, and the kitchen with an island and six-burner stove, where he'd cooked stir-fry in a wok for her on more than one occasion.

Privacy trees surrounded his ten-acre property, making it feel like a small, secluded slice of paradise. He'd worked on different rooms throughout their dating—some he did himself during downtime from Rider SI and some he'd contracted out. Now, she could appreciate the finished product, even though it saddened her to think they had no future together under this roof. If he was going to offer for her to live with him, he would have done it long before now.

Santino interrupted her thoughts when he slid a sandwich onto the table beside her laptop.

"Reece will be mad at me if I tell him you skipped a meal."

She arched an eyebrow. "I work twelve-hour shifts in the ICU. I skip meals all the time."

"Not on my watch."

She took a bite—an olive-heavy, warm muffuletta on ciabatta bread—and chewed slowly as she stared at him, unblinking, until the flavor forced her to close her eyes and enjoy it.

"Mmm. Thank you."

"Good. You find anything helpful?" He looked down at her chicken scratch on the paper. Some of her notes were related to the case, and some were just doodles.

"Maybe," she said around her bite of food before swallowing. "I feel like my brain is sputtering as it tries to make the connection, but I'm missing rungs on the ladder or whatever analogy a security team might use. A missing firing pin?"

"That works." He leaned over and looked at her computer screen. "That isn't the hospital site."

"No. I was looking at the FDA's registered drug trial site. I initially thought the entire list Lori sent me was comprised of patients who'd taken the street drug. But that isn't true. Some of the patients on the spreadsheet were on a study drug."

"Some but not all?"

"Not all. Not even half."

"So why is it relevant?"

"I don't know," she said softly, hating her own defeated tone.

Jess pushed away from the table and rolled her neck in a slow circle. "I've been sitting and staring at patient charts for too long. Can you do me a favor? Can you text the name Poindexter Pharmaceutical to Claire so she can learn more about them? I need to take a break."

"*Bueno*," he agreed, pulling out his phone. "Any context with it?"

"A drug called trihydrodone. Thanks."

When Jess walked down the hallway, Santino didn't follow. She passed the guest room and walked to the master bedroom. The color palate was a tasteful mix of fern green and gray with dark wood furniture. The back window overlooked Reece's acres of field rimmed with trees. Huh. The hot tub on the back porch was a new addition.

The quiet stillness of his property and surroundings created a serene ambiance. She walked through the bathroom, memories of times in the jacuzzi and the two-headed shower heating her core. The walk-in closet was now complete. To her surprise, it had his and her sides, with the woman's side being notably larger and containing a shoe section.

She entered the library and circled the perimeter of the large square room as she contemplated the meaning of Lori's data. Jess methodically assembled the facts as she understood them. All of the patients had a similar acute lung injury and had been admitted to the ICU. Some recovered, some didn't. Of the ones who'd had urine drug screens, all were positive for narcotics. Some had other substances in their system, but all of them had narcotics.

Coincidence, or no?

Since some had a history of drug abuse, narcotics weren't surprising. Since some had chronic pain, also not surprising. Other patients might have received narcotics during their emergency room visit prior to having a urine drug screen sent. So maybe no narcotic link existed.

When she'd first glanced at the data back at the Rider cabin, she'd assumed the patients had all taken Luminous, but on her detailed chart review, that theory proved false.

All of the patients who had a CRP—c-reactive protein—checked had elevated levels indicative of inflammation. But this was also not terribly surprising in the setting of acute lung injury.

Her mind grasped for that elusive rung of the ladder that would help her take the next step. How did sick ICU patients tie into Dr. Sullivan and also tie into Lautaro Fernandez?

When at last the piece materialized into place, an icy fist gripped Jess's heart. The terrible truth hit her hard and fast, causing her to lean against the chaise lounge in the library.

She shook her head and shuddered. No, the scandal she'd concocted to link the pieces had to be wrong. Had to be too far-fetched.

Too conspiratorial.

If she was right, then she'd just found the firing pin to a loaded weapon.

10

———

*L*autaro overturned the desk in front of him. Pens, paper clips, and stationary went skating across the floor.

Dom sat quietly in his chair, filing his fingernails. "Brother, your blood pressure."

Lautaro smoothed his dark hair back as he regained his composure. When he stopped seeing red, he realized he was in Dom's home office. Ah, well. He could buy him new furniture if needed. If his brother had bought a sturdy desk to begin with and not some cheap, self-assembled plywood, Lautaro wouldn't have been able to overturn it in the first place.

"A simple task—apprehend Dr. Ong and the USB—has failed. This doesn't bode well for my future distributions of Luminous." Lautaro had received additional details that someone highly trained had been responsible for thwarting his men's efforts to retrieve the USB and capture Dr. Ong.

"And then there are those two idiots who weren't supposed to kidnap anyone. They were supposed to kill the DEA agent." Lautaro seethed. He had sent his men to kill Special Agent PJ

Tuder, but instead they'd found his daughter with the babysitter. Unsure what to do, and probably idiotically thinking it would be helpful to Lautaro, they'd kidnapped the girl. More flies in the ointment.

Lautaro had tried to make the best of the situation by keeping her captive and threatening the DEA agent in order to keep his mouth shut. He wasn't sure how much the man knew about Luminous, but he'd been snooping around entirely too much.

Lautaro had been tasked with keeping the origins of the drug a secret—an exceedingly more difficult assignment as sales channels expanded throughout the country. It didn't help that the medical field was taking notice of the side effects.

"You know the saying, if you want a job done right…" Dom's voice trailed off.

Lautaro cast a side glance at his brother. Was Dom making a helpful suggestion or bating him into dangerous activity? He wanted to trust his brother, but if Lautaro was eliminated, Dom would be able to take charge of a lucrative empire. Dom didn't seem overly ambitious, but Lautaro could never be too certain. Caution seemed the better part of valor.

Lautaro clenched and unclenched his fist as he kicked office supplies out of his path with the toe of his leather Berluti Scrittos. "I've got a DEA agent who is still alive, another doctor who might threaten to blow the whistle like Dr. Sullivan"—fortunately other people in Chicago had dealt with her—"and a flash drive with God knows what damning information on it floating around out there."

"And you've already dispersed people to help with all of those things. Trust your leadership and your men. Give it a little time."

Cool, calm Dom. Easy for him to say because he wasn't in charge. He wore his tattered blue jeans and casually lounged on the sofa. Still, he was an asset to Lautaro. If he dispatched Dom to kill someone, the man never failed.

Lautaro was on the verge of pointing out to Dom that his men had botched recent tasks and so did not inspire confidence when his phone rang.

Putting the phone on speaker, he held it for Dom to hear. "What have you got?" Lautaro asked.

"We discovered the name from our Atlanta PD source of the man who attacked our men at Dr. Ong's apartment."

A glimmer of hope sparked Lautaro's interest.

The caller continued, "His name is Reece Owen. Former Army Ranger. Now he works for some company called Rider Security and Investigation. Word is—it's the same group Special Agent Tuder hired to rescue his daughter."

Lautaro glanced at Dom, who gave him a victory grin.

Former Army Ranger. That would explain how he had swiftly and successful counterattacked.

"So, what is his relationship with Dr. Ong?" Lautaro asked.

"Friends or lovers, *yo no sé*."

"*Bueno*, well done. Pay your informant for the information." Lautaro clicked the phone off and turned toward Dom. "Probably safe to assume this Reece Owen is hiding Dr. Ong and providing some protection."

Dom slowly pushed to his feet. "*Sin duda*. I'll find out where he lives and take a small group of men to snuff him out. We'll take out the woman and get the USB back." His tone sounded so simple, as though he were going to pick up bread and milk at the grocery store.

Lautaro envied his brother's calm disposition. *Madre mia*, if they were up against an Army Ranger, a few men might not cut it. "Take six men."

REECE OVERPOWERED JUAN'S getaway driver in the deserted alley behind the club. He bound and gagged him. Next, he slashed the tires of the other car parked behind Z Club.

He confiscated the keys and phone from the unconscious driver before sliding behind the wheel. With everything in place, he sent the messages he'd prepared moments ago, alerting the drug dealers to an impending, albeit nonexistent, police raid.

He set his gun within easy reach beside him and watched the rear exit door.

A tap sounded on the passenger side window. Reece jerked his head right and raised his gun. When he saw familiar blonde curls, he swore and lowered his weapon.

The last person he expected to show up outside a drug-dealing strip joint was his boss, Mica Rider. When he unlocked the door, she opened it and got in beside him.

"Mica, I could have shot you. You need to leave. Any minute, one of Atlanta's most ruthless drug dealers is going to burst through that door in a frenzy."

"Oh, I put together what you're up to," she assured him, all smiles and dimples. "What I don't understand is why you thought you had to do it alone."

Reece suspected Claire was tracing his whereabouts through the company phone. She probably figured out who owned the Z Club and alerted Mica.

He ran a hand through his hair. "These men are animals, Mica. They'll maim anyone who so much as dares to look at them cross. I didn't want to put any of the Rider team at risk."

He hoped his words wouldn't insult her. Mica possessed formidable hand-to-hand combat skills, and she could black-and-blue any Rider team member in a fair fight.

She gave him a withering look. "We just rescued a DEA agent's child who'd been kidnapped by Lautaro's men. I think we understand just how bad they are. We are all always at risk, and we strap on our weapons every day knowing that. I know how capable you are, and you've saved a lot of lives over the years, but you are not alone—never have been. And we sure as heck look after our own."

"Jess is—"

"Obviously one of our own, considering the way you're going off half-cocked and looking for trouble." Before he could protest, she said, "Swap places with me. I'll drive while you interrogate."

Reece swapped places as Mica grumbled about how his one-man self-assignment was going to get him killed. For a moment, she sounded like his former boss, Maxine Rider, though without the swear words.

She pulled her hoodie over her head to cover her blonde hair. At least Mica wasn't blocking his mission and demanding he leave. She intended to help him, for which he was grateful.

The back door of the club burst open and two Latino men, two black men, and two Caucasian men dashed outside. One of the Latino men and one Caucasian man dove into the back seat of the car Reece had confiscated. The other four dashed toward the second parked car.

The Latino, a rotund man in his fifties, clutched a briefcase as he shouted, "Go! Go!"

Mica, who already had the car started, accelerated.

Reece turned in his seat, raising his gun at Juan Penaloza and the manservant beside him. "Gentleman, if I may have your undivided attention for the duration of the drive, I have several questions that need to be addressed."

"Who the hell are you?" Juan demanded.

"I am the man holding you at gunpoint," Reece said, stating the obvious.

"What the hell do you want?"

Reece shook his head. "I have questions in need of answers. Honestly, are you even paying attention?"

Mica turned another corner and brought the car to an abrupt halt.

Reece pointed his gun at the man beside Juan. "Get out. Leave the briefcase with Mr. Penaloza."

The man glanced at Juan, who nodded. When he left, Mica locked the doors and drove again. She pulled onto the highway and kept to the speed limit.

Juan glared at Reece. "You're a dead man."

"We are all are dead men, eventually," Reece said casually.

Juan leaned back and regarded Reece carefully. Reece suspected the man's adrenaline flight response had dissipated enough that rational thought had returned, and he realized no amateur had orchestrated his captivity.

"Tell me about Luminous—suppliers, distribution, marketing plan."

Juan snorted. "Why would I do that?"

Reece blinked at him. "Because I'm threatening your life with a gun."

"If you kill me, you learn nothing."

"No. I learn nothing *from you*," Reece clarified. "Lautaro has, what, a few expendable men like you in every major city?" Reece shrugged. "If you don't tell me, I shoot you and move on to the next one."

Reece caught Mica glancing out of the corner of her eye at him as she drove. He took that as a good sign that his act was convincing.

"I don't know all the details," Juan began bitterly. "He's rolling out Luminous to Dallas next month. Every city has seen major sales. It's highly addictive, and people keep coming back for more."

"What is Luminous?"

"A narcotic. The most powerful in pill form—or so I'm told. Like oxycodone, people swallow the pill or crush it to snort or inject. What do you care anyway? You're obviously not a cop."

"Where is it manufactured? Colombia, Bolivia, Argentina?"

"Chicago."

"It's made in the US of A?" Reece didn't conceal his surprise—not only in the US but specifically Chicago, where Lori Sullivan had lived and died.

"Yes. That's one of the reasons Lautaro Fernandez loves it. No cost of international transport."

"Do you know anything about a Dr. Lori Sullivan—a woman recently killed in her hometown of Chicago?"

Juan shrugged. "I don't know this name."

"Okay. That concludes our Q and A session. Let's talk about next steps. You were just abducted in your own car behind your own club. Only you and I know the topic of our discussion, which thus far is not detrimental to you or Lautaro. But, I say again, only you and I know that. Your organization is going to speculate about how much lip service you gave to me upon threat of your life."

Juan's angry gaze bore into him.

"I'm going to drop you off somewhere which will free you from suspicion of wrongdoing. You won't thank me now, but you'll understand eventually. If you ever decide to retaliate against me or anyone close to me, I will use the resources at my disposal to uncover secrets Lautaro has and make it seem as though their reveal originated from you." He didn't make a habit of snatching and threatening drug dealers and Juan's retribution could come swift, but Reece needed to solve Jess's case in order to get her out of danger. If that meant putting himself in danger, so be it.

Mica parked the car beside a fire hydrant on Peachtree in front of the Atlanta PD headquarters. Reece holstered his gun in his blazer. Together, Mica and Reece took the keys with them as they walked away from Juan's car.

"The cop station was a good idea. Juan will be arrested for possession of drugs," Reece said. The way Juan had clung to the briefcase, it likely contained either drugs or cash, or both.

Mica nodded, squinting into the sun as she tugged off her hoodie.

He added, "It may be a temporary fix, but at least he won't be someone else to worry about while I'm helping Jess."

"The street drug is made in Chicago where Dr. Sullivan worked," Mica said.

"We already know the physician was tracking the ICU admissions related to those having taken the drug, but that doesn't explain what's worth killing for. If it's made in Chicago and she stumbled upon their manufacturing plant, I would hope she would have simply called the authorities. Knowing it's made in Chicago doesn't help us understand why she sent patient data to Jess. Jess is working to understand the data set as we speak."

"Perhaps she'll uncover something of value."

"Thank you for helping me, Mica."

Mica turned and looked him directly in the eye. "Keep me posted. This is officially a Rider case."

"Yes, ma'am."

11

On the drive back to his place, Reece flexed and extended his knuckles. They'd been scraped during his scuffle with Juan's driver, but the blood had dried. His mission had earned him some answers—and a sample of Luminous—but questions remained. Perhaps Jess had found something in her search, but he couldn't fathom how a spreadsheet could reveal the truth. He wished she would let Claire have a crack at it, since she might be able to find patterns not obvious to others. But Reece would respect Jess's passion for protecting patient information.

His mind drifted to thoughts of Jess. He recalled the first argument he'd ever had with her. She'd criticized his place one too many times, and he'd been fed up with it.

On a stakeout with Ryan Walsh later that day, he'd chewed irritably on a toothpick as he weaved his pocketknife through his fingers.

"You want to talk about it?" Ryan had asked.

From inside the car, they waited for Hoyle, one of Lucius Titan's men to emerge from a motel.

"No," Reece snapped. He hadn't even told Ryan anything had been bothering him. "Jess and I had a fight."

"First fight?"

"First one that made me mad enough to walk out. Everything else has just been bickering. I don't have the patience for female drama. I don't even know why I bothered dating Jessica."

"You don't?" Ryan arched an eyebrow.

"No, I don't. She's ridiculous with her high heels and enormous purses. She keeps boutique shops in business, that's for damn sure." He'd pegged her as soft and pampered when they'd first met at his best friend's wedding. Later, he'd come to understand that she'd scraped her way out of her parents' poverty and taken loans for college and medical school. Everything she had she'd busted her butt to earn. She worked long hours and took holiday shifts for colleagues who had children.

Ryan shrugged. "It's her money to spend as she pleases."

"That's what she says." Reece inadvertently bit the toothpick in half before tucking the pieces in his pocket to discard later. "All that makeup and fuss," he added.

"Is that what you fought about? Her extravagant tastes for the finer things in life?"

"No." She was beautiful when decked out in glamour, as when he'd first met her, and first thing in the morning without makeup —dark hair spilling over her smooth ivory skin. He didn't care about her expensive tangibles. He couldn't pinpoint what did vex him. "We fought about her criticisms of my house."

"It's a nice, big house, but it is kind of a bachelor pad."

His partner was taking her side? "I *am* a bachelor, Walsh."

"You've been meaning to clean up the place and finish remodeling some rooms."

"Yeah. And I don't need her breathing down my neck about it."

"Okay. Okay." Ryan raised his hands in surrender.

"Somehow, you manage to still sound like you're taking her side even as you say words of agreement." Reece grumbled.

Ryan sighed. "Do you think her complaints about your place might have some other meaning? Maybe she's expressing herself about one thing while avoiding approaching something else that's bothering her?"

"Shit, Ryan. Who has time for guessing games? If she's pissed about something else, she can't expect me to figure out what's bothering her. I'm supposed to have a crystal ball for this crap?"

"No, but you do investigative work for a living ..." Ryan's let his words hang in the air.

Reece shoved the pocketknife back in his pocket. "You think it's work related?"

"Do you think it's work related?" his partner countered.

Ryan's slightly patronizing tone grated on Reece's nerves. "She usually tells me when her day at work has been difficult."

"You've dated how long now?"

"Six months. With my work and her work, we only see each other a few nights every few weeks. I can't fix her work schedule, and I'm not quitting my job, if that's where you're going with this."

"I don't think she'd expect that."

"Good." Reece tapped his fingers against his blue jeans, fighting the restless urge to get out of the vehicle and take a walk. "Did I ever tell you she walked out on me in Antigua the first night we spent together?"

"You may have mentioned it once or twice. How many women have you left before sunrise after a one-night stand?" Ryan asked guilelessly.

Reece pursed his lips. Ryan's point was annoyingly accurate. Still, he'd thought the first night with Jess had been mind-blowing. The nerve of her to be the one to leave. Three had weeks passed before he'd reconnected with her, entirely intending another phenomenal one-night stand, ending with *him* leaving early. He had followed through on that plan, only to find himself wanting more and reconnecting with her a week later. She was as addictive as opium.

The third time, he'd stayed—even cooked her breakfast, which was when he'd learned she had an intolerance to lactose. The next time he'd promised himself he would tell her he needed distance, even though she'd never been demanding about when they would see each other next.

But when she came to his house vulnerable and distraught after a brutal night at work with an angry family member whose loved one had died, something in their relationship had shifted. Reece had listened to her talk about her amazing job and saw the depth and character of the woman he'd superficially judged. That day, he'd decided to try a relationship with her. A real one.

Reflecting on their dating now, as he drove his truck back to his house, he likened the last three years to the equivalent of trying to ride a dragon—all ups and downs, fiery temper and icy scales, thrashing and gnashing of teeth.

Worth it, he decided.

He just wished he'd come to that realization before he'd hurt her one too many times.

REECE PARKED his truck in his driveway beside Jess's car and strode inside his house. He made a mental note to charge her car tonight so it would have full mileage should they need to make another trip. He had installed a charger in his garage specifically for her car.

He greeted Santino, who met him in the entranceway. "Where's Jess?" He continued into the kitchen, where he pulled a pack of peas out of the freezer and covered the knuckles of his right hand in the cold relief.

"Library," Santino said. "You learn anything?"

"Maybe. Luminous is made in Chicago—same place Lori lived —and I got a sample of the drug. How is Jess doing?"

"Holding up. Said she needed a break, and she's been staring at shelved books for an hour." He tucked his hands in his pockets.

"I'll check on her," Reece said.

"And I'll head home. I'm not all about being a third wheel."

"Hey, Santino?"

"Yeah?" He hesitated on his way to the door.

"Thank you."

Santino shrugged. "We're partners." With that, he left.

Reece dropped the peas back into the freezer before walking to the library, eager to see Jess. He didn't know why. He'd only been away six hours, and before this fiasco started, he'd managed just fine for three months without seeing her.

Okay, that was a lie. He'd missed her terribly. And when he hadn't been on the job, he'd worked on his house—always asking himself what Jess would like. A library. A walk-in closet. A garage charger for her electric car. A hot tub—well, that might have been something for the both of them to enjoy.

When he entered the library, he could see her profile as she stared out the window. She looked small and pale.

"Jess, are you okay?"

"Reece."

The smile that lit up her face as she turned toward him weakened his knees. How was he strong in the face of men twice his width but made weak by one look from this woman?

"Reece," she repeated his name as she rushed into his arms.

She wrapped her arms around his chest and squeezed as if needing an anchor. He took her in his arms and buried his face in her silky hair. She smelled so good. He would have been content to hold her like this all afternoon.

After a moment, she arched up and pressed her lips to his, ravenous.

Shock and surprise stole his breath. Every part of his body revved with excitement. He knew too well the depths of pleasure their bodies were capable of creating together.

He picked her up mid-kiss, and she wrapped her legs around him as her fingers sunk into his hair. His mind sputtered as other parts of his body stole his blood supply and throbbed. Wasn't this the part where he was supposed to play the responsible adult and discuss boundaries and caution against choices made in haste?

Caution be damned. Jess wanted something, and he knew precisely how to give it to her.

He carried her to the bedroom—his bedroom—as his body relished the touch, feel, and smell of her. He was instantly aroused in a way his body had only ever responded to her.

"Jessica," he managed between kisses, but she never slowed as she peeled the clothes off of him.

Something had upset her, or perhaps she'd dwelled too long on the what-might-have-been at her apartment. Whatever had affected her, she wasn't ready to share. She was ready to escape. He could offer her that reprieve, but knowing the intimacy was temporary would cost him a piece of himself.

He surrendered to her anyway, giving himself over to her as he caressed and kissed every tantalizing place on her body. As he drove her deep into pleasure, she reciprocated, giving as much as she took. She was always amazing that way with lovemaking—giving and taking equally and holding nothing back.

Her skin felt smooth and cool as he ran his hand along her bare waist and up to her breasts. He would warm her. He would bring her to a boil until she screamed her release.

And he did.

When she finished, she gasped for breath but staved off collapse until Reece joined her in ecstasy, his world shattering as his body rode the waves of pleasure.

Then he held her tight, simultaneously wishing he could wipe her troubles away and grateful that her crisis had driven her back into his arms.

He would fix her dilemma, he vowed. But could he also reconcile their relationship? Did he have a right to? He didn't feel worthy of her—never had. Did that mean he should let her go—as he had before—or strive until he felt worthy?

Jess lay beside Reece, feeling his warm skin and the rise and fall of his chest against her cheek. Her left hand rested on his bare skin. She felt boneless and sublimely satisfied.

Clinically, she knew almost every muscle, bone, and blood vessel of the human body. She knew which nerve endings supplied the sensation to where her hand lay over his sternum. But emotionally, indulging in Reece's touch and feel rendered her nearly speechless.

She wanted to stay here forever, forgetting her troubles and the outside world. Reece's actions could make her feel more cherished than anyone ever had. She hadn't bothered to date when they were having one of their hiatuses from each other. Anyone she tried to date would fall short of her expectations when she compared him to Reece.

She always found her way back into his arms or he into hers. But never permanently. Wasn't the definition of insanity doing the same thing over and over and expecting a different result?

Not this time. This time she would expect more of the same. They had no lasting future, and she needed to go back to her home in Chicago. Isn't that why she'd never let it go and fully committed to Atlanta? She still paid the lease on her Chicago flat. Deep down, she knew he wasn't the type of man who would settle down for anyone. Such a notion clashed with his persona of independence—a man who needed no one.

His eyes were still closed and his breathing rhythmic. Even in sleep, his mustache twitched. What did a man like Reece Owen dream about? Chasing bad guys? Parachuting out of planes into enemy territory? Rescuing the damsel in distress?

Surely nothing so mundane as mere mortals might. Her happiest dreams had been reenacting moments with him—from excursions to steamy nights.

Her nightmares were finding herself back in college and late for an exam, or back in high school and somehow forgetting to wear pants that day. On rare occasions, she had nightmares about patients she'd lost. After this experience with the drug dealers, she would have all new nightmares, and Reece wouldn't be there to reassure her when those nightmares invaded her dreams.

Reece lightly stroked his fingers along her arm. She noticed the red knuckles on his right hand. She touched them gently before bringing his hand to her lips and kissing each raw knuckle.

"Did you learn anything?" she asked, knowing once they started on this topic, all intimacy would vanish.

"Supposedly, the origin of Luminous is Chicago."

"That supports my theory."

Reece pushed himself up in bed to rest on one elbow. "You have a theory?"

Jess sat up and pulled on her shirt, which had been discarded on top of the bedside lamp, and sat cross-legged near him. "I do. It scares the hell out of me, but it's the only thing that makes all the pieces fit." She slid out of bed and pulled on her Gucci blue jeans.

Reece frowned. "Telling me your theory does not obligate you to put on clothes."

"I need to do something with this nervous energy."

"I have ideas." He wiggled his eyebrows at her.

She granted him a slight grin but began brushing her hair. If they made love again, she'd start dwelling on the lack of a future relationship between them.

She cleared her throat. "So, the patients in Lori's database all had acute lung injury and all were either known users of illicit drugs or part of a drug trial. That's what the ILL or TRL column in the spreadsheet was for. Illegal or trial. The drug trial is for a new narcotic—trihydrodone—manufactured by Poindexter Pharmaceutical operating out of Chicago."

"Are you suggesting that Luminous and trihydrodone are the same drug causing the same side effects?" he asked.

She stuffed her phone in her back pocket and pulled on her Golden Goose white sneakers. "Yes." She paced the room. "But for that to be true, someone at the pharmaceutical company would have to be selling the medication to Lautaro Fernandez. They would be selling a narcotic—*not* approved by the FDA—to a drug dealer. That's mind-bogglingly illegal and immoral."

At Reece's unsurprised expression, she guessed he'd witnessed far more egregious acts of immorality.

Reece tossed the covers off and slowly got dressed. "If your speculation is true, then I suspect they're after a profit before FDA approval."

"Or before they get shut down altogether. The company will have to show their data, including adverse events. Poindexter Pharmaceutical must know about the acute lung injury from the drug. Drug companies are tasked with monitoring all patients for adverse effects. When the FDA sees an unusually high number of drug-induced pneumonitis and acute lung injury, the drug will not get approved. That's millions of dollars lost in research and development."

"Unless you turn a profit by introducing a potent, highly addictive narcotic to the illegal drug market." After jeans and a T-shirt, he pulled on his socks.

"Exactly." She let out a huff. "But, damn. I mean, to pull that off, you have to have somebody doctoring all of the books—raw materials, production, inventory, and output."

"Or two sets of books. And how do we prove it? Unless we force this into the light, Lautaro and whoever is pulling the strings at the pharmaceutical company will want to eliminate you once they get their greedy hands on that blasted USB drive."

"I need to prove it's the same drug. I need samples of both. A friend of mine could run mass spec on them to see if they're the same drug."

"Slow down. Slow down." He raised a hand in her direction. "I'd like to explore a solution that doesn't have you directly involved."

"I'm already directly involved," she protested, heat rising to her cheeks.

"More than you already are."

She put her hands on her hips. "You're going to sideline me while the menfolk handle it?"

"Jess—"

"Because I'm going to be a part of the process that sets me free. People are dying, and those who survive have permanent lung damage. As a physician, I'm not going to be idle while lives are at stake. I'm going to make sure it's done right."

"I'm part of an exceedingly competent team." Reece's tone grew a sharp edge as he tugged on his boots.

Before the heated discussion could continue, a chime sounded from another room.

Jess's heart thudded. "That's your driveway alarm."

Reece's face darkened. "Car on the drive. No one texted me they were coming."

Jess recalled Reece telling her the driveway had weight sensors to announce the arrival of guests—wanted or unwanted.

A second then third chime sounded.

"Three cars," she said, her mouth suddenly dry. A wave of flushing and vertigo struck her as if she'd taken a slug of his whiskey.

Reece was already strapping on his gun holster and pocketing his phone. He picked up his jacket on the way to the hall.

"Follow me."

12

Reece headed toward the library, Jess close on his heels. "Grab your laptop. Pack your things—one bag only, and keep it light. You have sixty seconds."

"Okay." She peeled off and dashed to the kitchen.

He appreciated her instant cooperation. She wouldn't allow him to sideline her from investigating the trial drug, but the threat of violence was Reece's realm. At least in this instance she was surrendering all autonomy and following his lead in the face of danger.

In the library, he used a keypad to open a compartment behind one bookshelf and pulled out an M24 SWS bolt action rifle and a box of bullets. He slung the rifle over his shoulder and made his way back to Jess.

She had her pink purse in hand, laptop inside. She pulled on her winter coat. Without speaking or panicking at the sight of his weapon, she followed him toward the back of the house.

As they exited from the back porch, he motioned for Jess to follow him into the field. Dry, brittle grass crunched under his boots as he strained to listen for sounds of men following them. The car engines were off, and only the cool wind rustling through the trees made noise.

Reece pulled out his phone and slipped in an earpiece as he speed-dialed Rider SI.

"Hello?"

"Claire, my place is under attack."

"Crap. What do you need? Reinforcements?"

"No, no one would reach us in time. Have Santino meet us on Sweetwater Road at Veterans Memorial Highway."

"What about local police?"

"You can call the police. They won't arrive here soon enough either."

"Fire department?"

"Yes, the sirens will be a nice distraction. But I don't want them getting shot. Call them as if you were driving by and saw guns and smoke from a distance so they don't hop out expecting a house fire and encounter gunfire."

Reece looked back at his house after their hundred-meter dash.

"My Tesla." Jess panted for air. She'd had to run to keep up with his light jog.

"We can't go back for anything," Reece told her.

"No." She pulled out her phone. "I have auto summons."

He stopped abruptly. "Tell me more."

"The new upgrade is four-hundred-foot range, but I have to have a line of sight from the car to my phone, and I don't think it will drive through a field. Also, it's slow—not like James Bond's autopilot in the movies."

Reece's mustache twitched as he pursed his lips. The open field offered no place to hide, and as soon as the men found the house empty, they could drive to Jess and Reece and overtake them. A tree line marked the boundaries, but it was shallow. By himself, he could outrun most adult men since he'd always been lean and ran track in high school. Jess was light, but she wasn't going to outrun anyone with her short legs.

"We split up." The idea pained and sickened him, even though it was their best chance of survival. "I'll take the tree line over there. You're on the opposite side of the house. I'll draw their fire." He unfurled his bullet-resistant blazer and wrapped it around Jess over her coat, since there wasn't time for anything else.

He extended his handgun to her. He had managed to coerce her into practice shooting twice while they were dating to learn the basics.

Her eyes went wide, but she took it—a big weapon for a tiny woman. If she didn't plant her feet as he'd taught her, she'd be knocked backward.

"Save your ammo," he instructed her. "You're not going to shoot anyone, but if they follow your car when you auto-summon it, shoot in their direction to buy yourself time to get in and drive away. Once you escape, circle around to Glenda Street to pick me up."

She adjusted the bag on her shoulder and said with mock incredulity. "Pick you up and risk my car getting shot at even more?"

Her unexpected humor caught him off guard. He grinned, planted a firm kiss on her lips, and dashed off to the far row of trees. When he glanced back, she was running in the opposite direction. Her pink bag was a damn bull's-eye, but Reece would make sure the assholes after her were focused on him.

Once he reached the tree line, he dashed over logs and between trunks to align himself with his driveway that circled in front of his house. Three men loitered by three cars haphazardly parked in his circle drive. He suspected the other men on their team had gone inside his house.

Amateurs.

A seasoned team would have sent two men along either side to meet around back and a two-man team through the front door. Instead, they'd simply assumed they had the element of surprise and stormed in through the front door only.

Reece found a broad-based tree whose trunk split six feet up. He moved a stump of another dead tree to the base so he could stand on it. Next, he positioned his rifle between the fork in the tree. He was three hundred yards from the vehicles.

Jess's Tesla started to move from where it was parked in the driveway in front of the garage. The men jolted at the sight and aimed their weapons at the empty car. They looked at each other in surprise. Before they could think to shoot out the tires, Reece fired.

One by one, he shot out a tire on each of their parked cars in his circle drive as the assailants dove for cover behind their vehicles. The Tesla kept its slow, steady drive toward Jess.

The men began firing in Reece's direction, the bullets from their handguns unable to reach him with any accuracy. One man spotted Jess and sprinted toward her. Reece shot him in the leg.

When three men came running out of the house shouting, Reece fired at his porch to keep them pinned down. This gave another man time to open the trunk of one of their cars and pull out a MAC-10 submachine gun.

At twelve-hundred rounds per minute, the attackers had the odds in their favor of hitting Reece or possibly pinning him down long enough to close the distance. However, since the magazine only held thirty-two rounds, they would run out of bullets two seconds after pulling the trigger.

Reece peered at Jess getting into the Tesla. She accelerated like a bat out of hell and disappeared. The pressure in his chest eased slightly.

He shrunk back, hiding behind the tree as more gunfire erupted in his direction. After slinging the rifle back over his shoulder, he stepped off the stump. When the MAC-10 clicked empty, he bolted, ignoring the pounding fear and loud, echoing gunfire from the other weapons.

HEART THUDDING, Jess left the gunfight behind her. She'd never been more thankful to own a car that went from zero to sixty in under three seconds.

Reece was now six against one. One deadly Ranger against six drug-running thugs. Now that she'd seen Reece in action twice, she almost felt sorry for the idiots. They didn't stand a chance.

Except Reece wasn't at war, and he wouldn't shoot to kill unless he absolutely had no choice—his life or theirs. The men he faced probably didn't have scruples like that.

He'd told her once that one of things he valued most at Rider SI was the nonviolent conflict resolution. Brains over brawn. And when violence was required, they tried to avoid anything lethal.

Jess let her foot off the pedal when Reece appeared at the side of the road. The regenerative braking quickly slowed the vehicle before she brought the car to a complete stop faster with the pedal. He slipped into the passenger seat, slightly winded but with an otherwise relaxed demeanor, not indicative of one who'd been running for his life. He set his rifle in the back seat. As soon as the door closed, she floored the accelerator. Reece scrambled to put his seat belt on.

He patted the dashboard. "Not a scratch on her."

"You were amazing," Jess said.

"You came up with the auto summons. My original plan had us running through the woods."

Heat spread through her at his simple compliment. She cleared her throat. "What was that weapon they pulled out? Was that a machine gun?"

"Basically, yes. And not a great one. It's an excellent weapon for a gunfight… inside a bus. Beyond that, it has no accuracy and runs out of bullets too fast."

"Can you help me out of this lead weight?"

He complied, and she was grateful to have his bullet-resistant blazer removed.

"Where to now?" she asked.

"Allow me to make a call." He dialed a number, then another and put his phone on speaker. "I've conferenced in Mica and Claire."

"Are you both okay?" Mica asked.

"The good news is we have escaped unharmed. The bad news is Jess's troubles are likely just beginning." He turned toward her. "Why don't you explain your theory to them?"

Jess told Mica and Claire about how Poindexter Pharmaceutical was conducting a trial on trihydrodone and might also be selling their experimental drug as a street narcotic—Luminous—to turn a profit. And how the drug was harming and even killing people.

"If it's causing harm, why don't they stop the trial?" Claire asked.

"Money," Jess replied. "Maybe they're hoping the adverse events will wash out with a larger sample size. Maybe they're keeping the trial going in order to cover the tracks of the missing drug."

"How so?" Mica asked.

"If they're willing to sell a drug illegally, I'd bet money they'd also be willing to falsify data."

Reece adjusted his long legs in the seat. "You mean enroll fake patients who appear to be taking the drug and consuming the supply?"

"Exactly. It wouldn't hold under data scrutiny but might be good enough on the surface to keep them in the black-market business until they get shut down by the FDA."

"What can you get us, Claire?" Reece asked.

"If you're asking if I can hack a pharmaceutical company's database remotely, yes, I can. But not in the timeframe we need it. Something like that would take me weeks."

Weeks. The word hit Jess like a gut punch. Her life had already been in danger twice in two days. How would she survive weeks being hunted? She glanced at Reece, knowing she couldn't do any of this without him.

She merged onto the onramp. He hadn't given her any direction on where to drive, so she took them south on I-85 and figured she could do the I-285 loop with her car on autopilot until they had a destination.

"We need someone on the inside," Reece said.

"Check Dr. Sullivan's contacts," she suggested. "Maybe she knew someone working at the company. To prove my theory, I'm going to need samples of both the trial drug and street drug to compare chemical composition."

Reece patted his pocket. "I have acquired a sample of Luminous."

"You did?" Jess asked.

"And I may have offended one of Lautaro's coworkers during my acquisition."

"Is that why they attacked your house? Because you went off half-cocked and stirred up trouble?"

"I admit, I may have caused trouble, but that hit squad arrived too fast to have originated from my shenanigans. Someone must have identified me after I rescued you at your apartment." He seemed unfazed by her accusation that he was somehow responsible for the attack.

Normally, digs like that would sour his mood. Not today. Jess wondered if that was because he'd been able to spend time in Ranger mode and shoot his gun.

No. He'd been afraid for her, and she'd never seen him afraid of anything. His imperviousness to her comment was surely because they were safe. For now.

Claire said, "I have an idea for a sample of trihydrodone. When Jess had Santino text me the pharma company name, I looked into their network of employees. One of the research representatives for the Southeast lives in Atlanta. What's more interesting is that I found an email from Lori to him asking for a meeting when work brought him to Chicago."

"Did they have that meeting?" Reece asked.

"Maybe. The guy, Scott Gumpert, flew out there three weeks ago, which was two weeks after she messaged him."

"We need to find out what they discussed and, you're right, see if he can provide a sample," Reece said. "Can you text me Scott Gumpert's home address?"

"Yes," Mica said. "But we'll also have Santino meet you there."

"I need a safe place to store Jess," he said.

She blinked at him. "I'm not a Tupperware container."

"No. You're Ming dynasty China, and I'm not risking you being in danger again." His phone pinged with a text, and he entered an address into the car's navigation system.

To cool her temper, Jess tried to balance the positive of Reece's statement—that he found her invaluable—against his implication that she was fragile.

With forced calm, she asked, "You and Santino will go into this guy's house and talk to him?"

He glanced at his phone. "If Scott Gumpert cooperates, we will talk to him. If he doesn't, coercion may be involved."

"And coercion can turn dangerous?"

He eyed her suspiciously. "That's correct."

"So, you might need a getaway driver."

Reece snorted. "You're not going to be our getaway driver."

"I'll be safely outside in the car. And you might need a fast getaway car like mine."

Mica interjected, "Reece, this is time sensitive. If you detour to take Dr. Ong somewhere, you'll lose time in Atlanta traffic. Your options are to take her with you, or I can assemble a different team—maybe Santino and Ryan—to meet Scott Gumpert."

Jess could feel the tension emanating from Reece, like heat off the Sahara Desert, even as she kept her eyes fixed on the road. He obviously didn't like his options. He clearly wanted to be the one to simultaneously fix Jess's situation and keep her safe, but he couldn't do both.

His jaw tensed. "Have Santino meet us there."

13

———

*R*eece let out a low whistle as Jess turned onto Peyton Road. "All half million to million-dollar homes."

"With all your renovations and your acreage, your house must be close to that," she said.

"Maybe if I add a pool." He glanced at her, wondering if she'd want a pool. He recalled the time they'd gone to the Four Seasons at Troon North and enjoyed the dining, hiking, and the pool. She had looked mouthwatering in her white bikini.

"So, how does this work? Do I pull into the driveway?" she asked.

"Park in front of Santino's Pontiac."

He had her block the end of Scott's driveway with her car intentionally in the event that the man tried to run. And if she needed to take off and gun it, no obstacles stood in her way.

As she parked, Reece checked his handgun. He turned in his seat toward her. "Keep your phone on in case you need to alert me of danger or vice versa. I'll tell you when to cut it back off. I need to know you'll stay here—even if you hear shouting or gunshots.

And I need to know that if there's trouble, you will leave." She started to open her mouth, but he continued, "We have Santino's car."

Before she could protest, he got out of the car and joined Santino on the curb. The man was dressed smartly in a Rider suit with his dark hair smoothly combed—unlike Reece who probably looked like he'd run through trees getting shot at by drug dealers. He brushed at his pants and patted his hair.

"Mica said to bring these." Santino handed him a Taser.

Reece smirked. He knew Mica's physician husband, David, encouraged them to find minimally violent resolutions to their conflicts. That only worked when the opposition played by the same rules. Still, he took the weapon and pocketed it.

Together, they walked up the sidewalk, past the manicured lawn, and to the front door—an oak with a double bolt framed in mortared stone. The house was three floors, probably four thousand square feet, with blended bricks of light and dark brown. It had a backyard with a wrought iron fence, low enough to leap over if needed. The short size also indicated no large dogs inhabited the premises.

Reece rang the doorbell. As he waited, he glanced through the rectangular window between the door and the stone to look at the home security keypad.

A figure moved behind the door. "Who is it?" His voice sounded strained.

"Mr. Gumpert, my name is Reece, and this is my coworker Santino. We work for a company called Rider Security and Investigation. We wanted to talk to you about Poindexter Pharmaceutical."

A face appeared in the glass, looking at them with wide eyes. He drew back from view. "You need to leave."

"We need to talk about your company. And we need to talk about Dr. Lori Sullivan."

A long stretch of silence ensued before the door slowly swung open. Santino moved to one side, his hand reaching for his weapon.

Scott Gumpert wore wrinkled flannel pajamas with red Santa hats that matched his bloodshot eyes.

He spread his arms. "Just get it over with."

Reece and Santino exchanged glances as Santino left his weapon holstered.

"Mr. Gumpert, may we come inside and talk?" Santino asked.

"You're not here to kill me?"

Reece frowned. "No." Reece entered, walking past the man, and scanned the foyer and living room for threats. The only threat appeared to be the overconsumption of alcohol, suggested by the empty liquor bottles on the table.

Santino closed the door behind him after he entered. "Why do you think your life is in danger?"

Gumpert rubbed his eyes. "Who did you say you were?"

"Private security company," Reece answered, passing blue sofas on a Persian rug and circling into the kitchen.

He wanted to ensure Gumpert was the only one in the house. Stainless steel appliances were interspersed among tall, white cabinets with distressed wood. In the center stretched a nine-foot island with a large sink.

Santino elaborated as they joined Reece in the kitchen, "We're investigating the death of Dr. Lori Sullivan." He passed a business card to Gumpert.

The man's shoulders sagged. "I can't believe she was murdered."

Reece's ears pricked. "Why do you think she was murdered? By all news reports, she died in a car accident."

"You're investigating." Scott tossed the card onto the counter. "You obviously suspect foul play, too."

Reece nodded as he found the cabinet with glasses and poured chilled water from the fridge dispenser. "We have our reasons. What are yours?"

Gumpert sank onto a bar stool as Reece passed him the beverage. "Lori reached out to me a few weeks ago about our study drug. I thought it was odd because she's not one of our researchers, but I referred her to the Poindexter representative in her territory. She said she wanted to meet me. She trusted me because she knew me from undergraduate."

"You went to the same college?"

He took a gulp of water and nodded. "University of Chicago. We were in the same organic chemistry class. I told her when I'd be in the Windy City and that could meet up with her then, but I warned her that I couldn't talk about a study drug—we all sign nondisclosures. She tells me, 'Don't talk, listen.' Very cryptic. So, I meet up with her, and I listened." He scrubbed his hands over the stubble on his face as he sighed heavily.

Reece sent a quick text to Jess as he listened, *All good in here. Scott is cooperating.*

She replied with a thumbs-up.

"Lori tells me this cockamamie story about our study drug being sold on the streets by drug dealers. I think, 'This chick has lost her mind,' but I listen because we're at this nice little café and my turkey and Swiss on rye is heavenly. Then, she opens her laptop and shows me her data." Gumpert took another gulp of his water. "I'm starting to feel compelled to believe her, but I still can't process what she's saying. I'm thinking, it can't be true." He sat, shaking his head.

"She wanted something from you," Reece prompted.

"She asked me for the company data." He gave a humorous

chuckle. "I'm not a researcher. I mean, the company doesn't give me access to the data—not that I would know what to do with it anyway. I do research oversight. I make sure institutions and individuals enrolling patients are following the protocols and reporting appropriately. The only numbers I get to see are when the company puts together cute little PowerPoint Web presentations with the data they've already analyzed. I can promise you there weren't an abnormally large number of patients with respiratory failure in the drug group compared to placebo in any of those presentations."

"What did she say when you told her you couldn't give her the data?" Reece asked.

Gumpert pushed away from the counter and began to pace. "She wanted a sample. Said she had a sample of the street drug she took off some kid who'd landed in her ICU after an adverse reaction. Said she needed a sample from me for comparison. But said I needed to hurry because she was starting to suspect someone might be following her." He shook his head slowly and laboriously, as if it weighed as much as a boulder.

"It's not your fault she died," Santino said, showing far more compassion than Reece felt capable of under the circumstances.

Gumpert's expression turned anguished. "Maybe I should have just given her the damn sample. I told her I needed time to think it over, and I flew back home. I ran away. Then she dies. Can't be a coincidence. I've been terrified ever since that I could be next—just for meeting with her and listening to her conspiracy theory. I haven't left home. I've been trying to figure out what to do next."

Reece considered Gumpert's circumstances. Since he'd met with Dr. Sullivan, he could be deemed by his company to be guilty by association. But instead of taking action, he'd stayed home and gotten drunk.

"Do you have any proof of what she told you?" Santino asked.

"No. And I suspect her proof died with her."

"Not all of it," Reece said. "What we have—combined with your testimony and that sample of the trial drug—will be the proof we need."

"Why do you care? Did you know Lori?"

"I never had the pleasure, but I do know a friend of hers who very much wants the truth to come to light."

Santino rested a hand on the man's shoulder. "Come with us, Mr. Gumpert. I'll take you to our downtown headquarters, and our team will protect you until the authorities can take over."

"You're going to get to the bottom of this?" the man asked with tentative hopefulness.

"We're committed," Santino assured him.

"A sample of the trial drug would be helpful," Reece added.

"I don't have any. I mean, it's never given to research reps. It gets shipped directly to the research teams from Chicago head-quarters. But we can stop by the hospital on the way. I have a good rapport with the Atlanta team."

"How fast can you throw on some clothes and pack a quick overnight bag?"

"I'll do that, but I'm not riding with you. I don't know anything about you or your company. You seem like decent guys, but I'm not getting in your car. And I'm not leaving my Porsche here. It goes where I go."

"Fine. It's no problem. We'll escort you," Santino said amicably.

Gumpert turned and left the kitchen.

When Reece heard his footsteps on the stairs, he turned toward Santino. "Watch him. I'm going to go update Jess."

"You think he's on the level?" Santino asked.

"Scott? I think his fear is real. But he may decide to bolt once he's inside that precious Porsche of his."

"Tracer?"

Reece nodded. "You have one in your car?"

"Yeah." He tossed Reece the keys. "If you grab it, I'll discretely plant it in his bag."

By the sound of the love affair the man had with his car, they ought to put the tracer there. But if Scott ran, he might realize the car would be the first identifying object he needed to disassociate himself from. He was more likely to keep his bag of clothes.

A cautious hope bloomed in Reece. If Rider SI could get the FBI and FDA involved based on Gumpert coming forward, whoever was after Jess would have to divert attention to dealing with an official investigation and perhaps abandon their pursuit of her.

***

JESS PERKED up when she saw Reece approach her. He went to Santino's car first and retrieved something.

When he neared her, she rolled down the passenger side window, and he leaned in.

"Mr. Gumpert is cooperating," he told her. "He thinks he can get his hands on the sample we need. We're going to follow him to the hospital, and then he'll follow us to Rider SI."

She bobbed her head. "Okay. That sounds promising." A tiny ray of hope struck her heart at his words.

"Sit tight. We'll be back out when he's done packing."

"Listen, Reece. I'm grateful for all your help. I know I've been hard on you." She gripped the wheel, thinking how an end to the case meant an end to their time together. Bittersweet—except maybe no sweet component existed.

He leaned into the car. "Come here."

As she leaned toward him over the passenger seat, he took her chin in his hand and kissed her. "We'll get you through this."

He stared at her a beat longer, and for a brief moment she thought he might say those three little words she ached to hear. But she wouldn't say it first as a ploy. He would have to say the words of his own initiative. Although his facial expression was one of love, she'd been so physically and emotionally drained from the last two days that she didn't trust herself to correctly interpret the soft compassion on Reece's face.

When he leaned back and turned toward the house, she rolled up the window to keep the warmth inside the car.

Suddenly, an explosion shook the vehicle and threw Reece backward, into her car. His body fell out of her view as debris rained down on and around the Tesla. Smoke billowed from what was left of Scott Gumpert's house.

"Reece!" she screamed.

14

With her ears ringing, Jess fumbled to open the driver's side door. Before she could press the button to get out and check on Reece, he slapped a hand against the window as he stood.

"Go!"

Leave him? That didn't seem right, and yet he had told her she had to leave if the situation turned dangerous.

"Get out of here now!" he bellowed.

In all their years of dating, he'd never given her an absolute command like this. If she didn't go, would she put him in more danger by making herself a target—someone he had to expend time and energy to defend? Would she be a distraction? Would she be his downfall?

She put the car in drive and accelerated, tears streaming down her face. How could he force her to leave him like that?

When she looked behind her, she saw him heading toward the house. She could see now that half of the structure was still standing. But for how long?

She wiped her eyes as she called Claire.

"Hello?"

"Claire, it's Jess."

"Are you okay? What's wrong?"

"Gumpert's house. It just exploded."

"Is anyone hurt?" The sound of Claire typing on keys emanated through the speakers.

"I don't know about Santino and Gumpert. They were inside at the time."

"Okay. Where are you?"

"In my car."

"Okay. Good."

"Reece made me leave. I think he's going back inside the burning house for his partner."

"Don't go back, Jess. I'm bringing Mica in on the call."

Jess waited with bated breath, still berating herself for abandoning Reece.

"This is Mica," the head of Rider SI said.

"I've got Jess on the line," Claire said. "There was an explosion at Gumpert's house. Sounds like Reece is alive, but that's all we know. Jess got away." As Claire spoke, Jess worked to regain her composure.

"Jess ran away" is more like it, she thought.

"Explosion?" Mica asked.

"Half the house is gone," Jess said.

"From inside or outside?"

"I don't know." She took a left, trying to circle the neighborhood from a distance. "No one was lurking around with a rocket launcher, but I don't know the difference between an inside bomb or one of those drone bombs. How did Lautaro even know we'd be at Scott Gumpert's house?"

"Assuming it was Lautaro," Mica said. "Walk me through what happened before the bomb exploded."

"We parked outside his house. Reece and Santino went inside to talk to Scott Gumpert. A few minutes later, Reece texted me that Scott was cooperating. A few minutes after that, Reece came outside to tell me Scott was coming with us for protection and would provide a sample of trihydrodone. He turned to walk back inside, and the house exploded. Well, half of the house."

"If someone was listening in, maybe that prompted the hit," Claire said.

"Still," Mica countered, "things have escalated quickly—from a two-man attack at Dr. Ong's apartment, to six thugs at Reece's house, to a bomb at Gumpert's place. Each one is a new level of danger... and professionalism. Even if someone was eavesdropping, how could they attack so quickly?"

"Reece is calling! I'm connecting him," Claire said. "Reece, Jess and Mica are on the call."

"I'm in the Pontiac with Santino."

"Is he okay?" Mica asked.

"A little smoke inhalation, and I hope not permanent hearing loss."

"I'm fine," Santino said, though Jess detected strain in his voice.

"Why don't we meet up? I can check him out," Jess suggested. Relief that the two of them were safe gave her a jolt of energy.

"Okay," Reece said. "Meet us at the CVS across from Terri's Café on MLK Junior Drive."

"What happened?" Mica asked.

"Santino says car bomb in Gumpert's Porsche. It activated when Gumpert started the car."

Jess consider Reece's words as she replayed the explosion in her mind. Yes, it made sense that it was actually the garage that exploded, taking part of the house with it.

Santino added, "He didn't give us a chance to sweep his car. He went upstairs to pack and came back down, sneaking around me to bolt for his car. I think he was going to run from us. Not that it matters now."

"Car bomb. That's promising," Mica said.

Jess shook her head, certain she'd heard wrong. "Promising? Why is that promising?"

Reece answered, "Gumpert's been holed up in his house for several days, so the bomb could have been planted five hours ago or five days ago, which means no one knew we were going there and maybe nobody knows we were. It was activated because he started the car, not because he was consorting with us."

"But we're back to not having proof of the scandal." Jess practically deflated in her seat.

No one responded to her statement, which she took as their agreement and a reflection of how dismal the situation remained.

"What about fallout?" Mica asked.

"I wiped prints as we left. Certainly neighbors could have spotted us—and any home outdoor cameras."

"Claire and I will deal with that. You get Santino to Jess."

WHEN JESS PULLED into the parking lot, she rushed to Santino, who sat in the passenger side of the Pontiac. She wanted to run into Reece's arms and give him a hug followed immediately by a tongue-lashing for making her leave, but she had a patient to evaluate.

She ran through a series of standard medical questions about Santino's injuries, his current symptoms, and if he ever lost consciousness. She inspected his pupils, cranial nerve reflexes, and anywhere he noted pain.

"What do you think?" Reece asked, having been pacing the parking lot the entire time and fumbling with what looked like a shattered Taser. Puffs of steamed breath twisted in the cold air around his head.

She took a step back from Santino and turned toward Reece. "He's okay. He's lucky." She had evaluated and treated trauma patients during her training but never blast victims from bombs. "Not even a concussion. What about you?"

"I'm fine."

She wanted to remind him that he'd body-slammed her car forty minutes ago and was not fine, but the harshness of his words kept her quiet. Maybe he was being tough for her or maybe for Santino. She wouldn't force him to show weakness in front of his partner, if that's what he was trying to avoid.

All three of them climbed into the warmth of Jess's car to call Mica and Claire back and sort out their next move.

"Ryan's on his way to you," Mica said.

"We need a new plan," Reece said.

Jess both admired and hated his perseverance. His body needed a break after that beating, but he wanted to keep pushing forward—for her. They seemed perpetually one—or more—steps behind unfolding events, so she understood the only way out of this was relentlessly through it. No pauses.

"We might have a plan," Mica said.

Claire said, "While you all were with Gumpert, I ran Dr. Sullivan's social media interactions against anything related to Poindexter Pharmaceutical. Looks like she was Linked-In associates with a Dr. Richard Zabner—a researcher employed by the drug company."

"That was fast," Jess marveled. "Where does Dr. Zabner live?"

"Chicago. He works at the company's headquarters."

Jess's mind churned with possibilities. "There are plenty of direct flights from Hartsfield to O'Hare. We can be there in a few hours. We can meet him and convince him to give us a sample of the drug."

"We?" Reece arched an eyebrow. "You are not venturing into the lion's den."

"Hello?" she fired back. "We're already in the lion's den, although I think Minotaur's Labyrinth is a better analogy. And we're being attacked by the damn bull. And a damn car bomb!" They seemed lost in a spiral of mazes with gunmen, bombs, and danger lurking around every wrong turn.

Santino sat quietly in the back seat, watching their exchange as he rubbed his jaw and opened and closed it as if testing it for functionality.

"Technically, *Daedalus's Labyrinth* held the Minotaur, but I'm not going to argue analogies with you," Reece said. "You're not going to Chicago."

"I don't recall asking your permission. This is my life and my situation, and I'm going to see it through to resolution." Jess programmed the touch screen to find the shortest route to the airport from their location. "People are dying because of this drug. I'm going to help put a stop to this."

Reece's voice grew seething. "Over my dead—"

"Um. Hello?" Claire chimed in sweetly. "Yeah, we're still on the line here."

Reece kept his cold glare on Jess, but she remained unflinching to his intimidation tactics.

"I have to agree with Dr. Ong on this one," Mica said. "She may be the best person to approach Dr. Zabner and secure his cooperation, especially since she was colleagues with Dr. Sullivan."

Any satisfaction Jess might have gleaned from winning a head-butting competition with Reece dissipated at his anguished expression. Ultimately, they both wanted her safety secured, but she wouldn't be locked in an isolated room waiting for this colossal scandal to blow over.

"We need an address and phone number for Dr. Zabner. And tickets from Atlanta to Chicago," he growled and disconnected the call.

AFTER MICA HEARD the line go silent, she called Claire.

"Did he just bark orders at me and then hang up?" Claire demanded. Through her irritation, Mica heard the hint of worry.

"He's emotional because he's afraid for Jess," Mica said as she fed Allen an afternoon snack of mango in his highchair.

"I get that, but he's not seeing logic. If his girlfriend gets a sample of the trial drug, she can identify if it's the same as Luminous. We call that a smoking gun. It makes sense for her to go."

"She's been in danger three times now, which has probably shaken him more than he cares to admit." Mica handed her son another chunk of mango, his face and hands smeared with the sticky orange fruit. Fortunately, she was using her earbuds so she wouldn't get her phone messy. Allen stuffed the fruit in his mouth and then tossed his sippy cup on the floor.

"When you go into danger," Claire shot back, "David doesn't get all '*Me Tarzan, you Jane*' on you."

Mica grinned, unfazed by Claire's irritation. Her frustration was also a reflection of worry—for the safety of Reece and Santino.

"David worries," Mica said. "But you're right, he doesn't manifest his worry as anger. But my husband knows I'm trained for danger. Reece knows Jess isn't."

Mica heard Claire typing on her keyboard, and she suspected the computer guru was already reserving the plane tickets Reece had requested.

"Then he needs to be her armor of Achilles, not confine her to the Isle of Delos."

"Armor of Achilles?" Mica asked, picking up Allen's cup and placing it back on his high-chair tray.

"I don't know." Claire sighed. "They were making Greek mythology analogies with the Minotaur thing, so I tried to match. Drake is a big Greek mythology fan."

"Except Achilles died young."

"Okay. Not my best reference. How about: Reece needs to be Jess's forcefield?"

"I like forcefield. I'd like my own forcefield."

"Why? What's wrong?" Claire asked.

Allen tossed the cup off the highchair again and squealed as if making his mother fetch a cup was the funniest thing in his life. Mica bent and retrieved it again, but before she handed it back, she gave him a disapproving look, which he thought was hilarious and laughed even louder.

"I need to go probe Lucius's brain on this one." Mica had already arranged for the visitation tomorrow morning. "I need to know how far we're liable to get lost in Daedalus's Labyrinth before this is all over."

"Mommy!" Allen blurted out with delight as he tossed the cup onto the floor again.

Claire groaned. "My skin crawls at the mere mention of Titan's name. I wish we had a different contact."

"Underworld contacts are all shady. At least this one is already behind bars."

Lautaro panted as he clutched the baseball bat and surveyed the devastation in the room. He'd smashed everything in the kitchen in a full 360-degree radius. Shattered glass, splinters of wood, and broken ceramic littered the floor. At least he'd been at one of his fronts for money laundering when Dom arrived with the bad news and not his own place.

"Lautaro, your blood pressure," Dom cautioned.

The violence had felt cathartic, but he still had to tell Shoup that the physician had escaped. Again.

Six men. Lautaro had sent six men to Reece Owen's home, and they'd returned empty-handed. Now all he had were three shot-up vehicles and his brother with a bullet through his leg that was currently being bandaged by Lautaro's medic.

"They must have known we were coming," Dom said, gritting his teeth as the wound was cleaned.

"An ambush?"

"I'm embarrassed to say I think it was just the one man."

"One man did this?"

"One Ranger and his rifle," Dom admitted with reluctance in his voice. "We thought we had the element of surprise. I should have parked to block their vehicles and distributed the men differently."

Lautaro paced as his brother's wound was bandaged. Two men had been shot in the span of two days—one at the physician's apartment who was now in police custody—and Dom at the cowboy's house. "No one does this to a Fernandez and lives to tell about it."

"On the bright side, Miguel finally got to fire his mini-gun."

Lautaro grunted in disgust. "I told him that thing was a waste of money."

Dom snorted. "Couldn't hit the broad side of a barn. Looked cool though. *Muy macho.*"

Lautaro rolled his eyes. "*Macho* is only of use if it gets the job done."

Dom grimaced as he flexed and extended his calf muscle. The bullet had taken a chunk of skin and would leave a nasty scar.

"You need some pain medication?"

"Like that garbage you sell? *Diablos no*. That crap can cripple you if it doesn't kill you."

Lautaro chuckled. It was deadly—deadly if consumed and deadly by association. But the consuming public didn't know this. Even if they did, would it stop them? People still vaped knowing it caused lung injury. People still snorted and injected cocaine, knowing it ravaged the heart and could cause stroke. *Everyone thinks they're immune*, Lautaro thought. Or maybe playing Russian roulette was part of the thrill.

He had a feeling the body count would only continue to rise. As long as it wasn't his team members dying and as long as he kept making money, he wouldn't worry about the body count.

He pulled out his phone and called Shoup. He instantly sobered when the man answered the phone.

"Hello?"

"It's Lautaro. We were unable to capture the physician or the USB." He'd been assigned this job because the physician was living in Atlanta, and he was currently staying in the city, overseeing the distribution of Luminous to a new market there. The failure didn't bode well for his future interactions with the company.

"I suspected not, since her name popped up on our search as having reserved a seat on a flight to Chicago," Shoup said, his voice its usual icy calm. He had a flat American tone with no obvious regional accent.

Lautaro swore.

Shoup added, "I'm betting she's not coming home to see dear old Mom and Dad, but to finish what Dr. Sullivan started."

Lautaro listened to Shoup's words as he paced, glass and debris crunching beneath his shoes.

"I can bring a team to Chicago," Lautaro began.

"Oh, I think you've been useless enough. You stick to drug distribution, and we'll handle the cleanup work."

Lautaro knew killing was Shoup's men's area of expertise. As was any covert work. This was why someone at Poindexter Pharmaceuticals had hired them in the first place—discretion. Still, he didn't like being discredited as worthless. And he would have his revenge for Dom's injury.

Before Lautaro could object, the call disconnected.

He glanced at his brother, who watched him carefully as he sat on a wooden bench with his leg elevated.

"*Si, bueno*," Lautaro said into the phone as if the call were still ongoing. He needed to save face. He couldn't simply be dismissed like that.

He pretended to disconnect the call before pocketing his phone.

"I'm going to Chicago to handle this personally. *Si quieres algo hecho bien, hacerlo por ti mismo.*"

If you want something done right, do it yourself.

"I'll go with you," Dom offered, making a show of attempting to stand on one leg.

"No, I need you to stay here and oversee distribution."

He could still find Dr. Ong and silence her. He could still put a bullet in Reece Owen as payback for his brother. Lautaro had an inside man in the Shoup Group, so perhaps he could stay one step ahead of Shoup and reveal his genius when he succeeded before they could.

15

---

*R*yan Walsh pulled into the parking lot, and Reece walked over to greet him.

"Santino's okay?"

Reece nodded. "He was in the living room when the blast went off. Knocked him senseless for a few minutes, but Jess checked him out. He's okay."

Jess joined them, and Ryan bent to give her a hug. "Good to see you," she said.

"I'm sorry you're going through this, Jess."

She gave him a weak smile. "At least I have the best team on my side."

Reece marveled at her resilience while simultaneously hating her situation. All he could do for her was push through until they found a solution.

Ryan turned to Reece. "I'll go with you to Chicago."

Jess interjected, "Actually, I was hoping you would take Santino for an ER evaluation and CT scan of his head."

"I'm fine," Santino grumbled as he joined the three of them.

"Just to make sure," Jess told him before turning back to Ryan. "If David is working, maybe he can facilitate."

"I'll take care of it," Ryan said.

"Thanks. And tell Jenna I'll call her when I can."

"Can I tell her you're okay?"

"Hey, I'm not the one who bounced off a car today." She shot Reece a pointed look as if to say she knew he was hurting and refused to admit it.

Reece gave her a bland expression in return. He'd slammed the passenger side door hard enough to knock the wind out of him and shatter the Taser in his back pocket. He was hurting, but it would pass. If he didn't know how terrible the narcotics were in his pocket, he'd be tempted to take them.

"I've got some ibuprofen in the SUV," Ryan offered.

Reece followed him a few steps away, and Jess seemed to take the hint that the two of them were going to speak privately. She gave Santino a hug goodbye and climbed back into her Tesla.

"What's up, Walsh?"

"Updates. We didn't unearth anything in our inquiries to Ernesto Busta which you haven't already found. Dorian learned the same thing you all have—Luminous is the latest craze in street drugs, and it originates in Chicago."

"It's good to corroborate the truth from multiple angles."

"Mica is going to tap Lucius for information tomorrow."

Reece pursed his lips. He hated to think of any Rider employee having to visit that snake. He knew Ryan detested it too. Ryan had, after all, worked for the pond scum of a man until he realized the lack of morality in Titan Enterprises. And he'd lost a friend to Lucius's ruthlessness.

"I suppose it was naive of me to think putting Titan behind bars meant we didn't have to deal with him anymore," Reece said.

Ryan nodded. "We all hoped that. He proved useful on Billy's case with Ethan Storm. Maybe he'll be useful here."

"I don't see how. Now that we know Poindexter Pharmaceutical is behind Luminous, we just need to prove it. If Lucius can somehow get us a sample from behind bars, I'd be impressed."

"I'll keep you posted." Ryan gave him a pat on the shoulder.

It was the closest thing they did to showing support for each other, and Reece was grateful for the gesture. Part of him wished he had his partner on this mission, but it was just a quick visit to a civilian. Yet Reece feared this Chicago trip could turn as complicated as the "simple" visit to Scott Gumpert's house.

REECE DIDN'T FEEL at ease until he and Jess were checked through security. Claire had gotten the two of them the soonest flight available, but it still left them with two hours to kill.

He felt unarmed and vulnerable, since he had to stow his weapons in her car, which they left parked in the airport lot. Fortunately, Rider SI had enough business in Chicago to justify keeping a stockpile of small weapons and gadgets stashed for easy access.

During their wait for the flight, Jess shopped for toiletries and a few outfits since they hadn't had time to pack before fleeing his house. She had told him she could skip the shopping and pick up clothes from her place in Chicago, but Reece didn't think it was safe to go there—not until Poindexter Pharmaceutical was exposed.

"The shop a few doors down has luggage. We'll buy you a carry-on," he said.

She had her pink purse over one shoulder and a stack of clothes draped over her arm.

She glanced up at him. "Is that your not-so-subtle way of telling me to keep my shopping spree small?"

He shrugged. "It's your money to spend as you see fit, but I would be most appreciative if it would all fit in a carry-on so we don't have to wait on baggage claim."

From weekend trips they'd taken together, he was unceasingly amazed at how she never packed light. Even though her clothes didn't occupy much space, by the time she'd packed a plethora of shoes, toiletries, and a hair dryer, she'd already exceeded carry-on capacity.

Rather than take offense, her expression held amusement. "Carry-on only," she assured him.

He bent down to kiss her cheek. "I'm going to pick up a few things for me. If I finish first, I'll come back here. If you finish first, meet me at our boarding gate."

When he straightened, his back reminded him he'd used Jess's Tesla as a backboard during the explosion at Gumpert's house, and the anti-inflammatories from Ryan had only made a dent in the pain.

He bought phone chargers, snacks, water, and ibuprofen in a convenience shop. In an adjacent clothing store, he purchased a heavy winter coat, hat, and gloves.

Now that Reece could breathe easier knowing Jess was momentarily safe, he was free to ponder their relationship. She was beautiful first thing in the morning wearing pajamas or all decked out for a night on the town. If they lived through this and were allowed the opportunity to share a life together, he would let her do whatever made her happy.

He would do things differently if given a second chance. He would still tease her about excessive luggage and how she always overdressed for the occasion, but there would be no real irritation in his comments. As long as she was his, she could pack as much as she wanted—when they weren't on an active case—and wear whatever tickled her fancy.

Jess might have owned a stylish car and expensive clothes, but she wasn't naive. She worked in the trenches of the ICU, putting tubes in every human orifice to save lives and covered in blood after procedures. She knew success and failure, life and death, victory and defeat.

She was no powder puff, even if she liked the powder and liked the puff.

She used to open up to him about her life in the trenches of medicine at the end of a shift—a patient who took a turn for the worse, a family member with unrealistic expectations, or a tragedy that she berated herself over what she should have done differently. She never mentioned patients' names or ages in order to maintain confidentiality, but he was certain she remembered every one of them.

Because of her resilience, she was managing her current predicament with admirable poise. Reece would do everything in his power to keep her safe, even though he couldn't shake a foreboding feeling that the worst was yet to come.

WHILE THEY WAITED to board the plane, Jess listened to Reece fire off pharma facts he'd found on an internet search on his phone: Chicago was the second largest pharmaceutical hub in the US with over fifty-two-thousand jobs and large corporations like Abbott, Baxter, Sigma-Aldrich, and Takeda. The city boasted almost nine million square feet of lab funding and seven hundred million dollars in National Institute of Health funding.

She leaned her head on his shoulder with her feet propped on her new—and very small—piece of luggage as Reece talked, his voice a deep, soothing drawl.

Was this the sensation when you finally accepted a relationship wasn't meant to be and you just enjoyed what little time you had together? Petty arguments like overpacking turned into cute quirks?

She'd found three outfits at the airport store, but her heart wasn't in shopping. Even one of her favorite activities couldn't distract her from what lie ahead—proving Lori Sullivan's theory.

Reece pulled out his phone and handed it to Jess. "You should call Jenna. She's concerned about you."

Jess frowned as an invisible weight bore down on her shoulders. She wanted to talk to her friend and felt touching base was past due, but first she gauged her own ability to remain emotionally in control.

She glanced around the busy terminal. People were crowded into the chairs while more strolled down the central walkway—some briskly to catch the next flight and others leisurely as they checked gate numbers or ambled in and out of stores. She wondered how many were on their way to their Christmas destination. Probably none of them were thinking about drug dealers, car bombs, and deadly medications.

Safe in the airport, Jess found her resolve. She took the phone and called her friend. Had she really seen Jenna less than forty-eight hours ago? The passage of time felt longer.

"Hi, Jenna, it's Jess." She pushed up from the seat so she could pace near the window and watch the planes taxi.

"Jess! I've been so worried about you."

Jess snorted to cover the angst tearing at her insides. "At least it's not like I owe the Cuban mafia twelve million dollars."

Jenna's situation a few years ago had seemed just as bleak then as Jess's did now, and the fact that Jenna had survived gave Jess hope for her own predicament.

"You've got the best team on your side," Jenna assured her.

"You're just saying that because you're sleeping with one of them." Snark was all Jess had holding her together.

"Ryan is my husband. And don't tell me you're not putting this opportunity with Reece to good use."

"Maybe I am. Maybe it's a bad idea."

"Maybe it's a chance to finally acknowledge that you two are meant to be together."

Jess glanced back at Reece who casually people-watched in the airport and was out of earshot of her conversation with Jenna. "He's in his element, on a case. When this is over, he'll remember all the reasons he's been pushing me away over the years."

"He might realize how unimportant those reasons are next to being with you."

"Look. I can only focus on one thing at a time. No multitasking." She appreciated Jenna's efforts, but she didn't want to allow herself false hope. "We're going to fly to Chicago, meet with someone Lori knew who works at Poindexter Pharmaceutical, convince him to help us, and then out the evil pharma company for selling their deadly product on the black market to turn a profit." Assuming Zabner cooperated and wasn't in on the scandal… and wasn't blown up by a car bomb.

"Be careful."

"Of course." Jess forced calm and a little cheer into her voice. "After all, I have my own personal bodyguard. Hey, can you ask around work about getting my shifts covered? Even if this is over tomorrow, I'm going to need some emotional recovery time."

"I'll take care of it."

"Thanks."

"Call me tomorrow," Jenna demanded.

"Okay."

Jess disconnected the call with her friend and checked the time. Boarding would start in twenty minutes. She wanted to hear one more voice.

"Hi, Mom."

"Oh, Jessica. Did you eat the dumplings?"

She cringed. They wouldn't be salvageable by the time she returned back home. "Not yet, Mom."

"Your father and I were talking about Christmas dinner. We'll make turkey, dumplings, rice, honey chicken, and pecan pie. Jay's wife is bringing tamago omelet with all those vegetables you like."

Jess smiled, thinking of their mix of American and Chinese food during holidays.

"Li is thinking of coming," her mom added.

Laughter threatened to bubble up in Jess. "I'm not going to date Li, Mom."

"Are you bringing someone?"

She looked at Reece, who was watching her now. He could probably tell by her posture and facial expressions when she was speaking on the phone with her mother.

"No, Mom. I'm just bringing my winning personality." She'd invited him once to meet the parents, and that hadn't gone well. She couldn't imagine inviting him to her house to meet her parents for the first time *at Christmas*.

"Not so winning, since you can't find a man."

Jess shook her head and couldn't suppress a chuckle.

"Are you laughing?"

"Yeah, Mom. I'm laughing." Jess had stewed so many times when her mom pestered her about finding a match.

Not today.

In the span of forty-eight hours, Jess had been fighting or running for her life three times. She'd been in the throes of passion with a man emotionally unable to commit to her, only to watch him get thrown against her car in her first ever witnessed car bombing and thinking he'd been severely injured. Her mom badgering her about dating felt blissfully normal.

"I love you. And I'll see you at Christmas," Jess said.

"Text me. If you don't bring a man, I'll provide one. Jay and his family are coming."

Jess loved her brother, Jay, but her mother always compared Jess against Jay's beautiful family with children. Suddenly, Jess wanted more than anything to be at Christmas with her mom talking about her next blind date, her dad nodding his agreement as he picked the pecans off the top of the pie and ate them, and Jay giving her an apologetic shrug as he tried to change the subject to his latest journal article or the kids' latest scholastic achievements.

"Okay." She chuckled again. "Thanks, Mom."

After she disconnected the call, Jess handed the phone back to Reece and boarded the plane with him. She watched the plane taxi and take off out of the small window with Reece beside her. She leaned against him and closed her eyes.

16

$\mathcal{R}$eece carried Jess's suitcase through Chicago O'Hare after they landed. She walked beside him as they navigated the terminal through the throng of people.

He checked his phone. Mica and Claire had texted to let him know Reece's place had been cleared out—the villains had evacuated when the fire department arrived. The fire department, finding no fire, had left. Mica had explained events to local police —someone had broken into Reece's house while he was away. They took shell casings and tire marks into evidence, and Reece would have to meet with them when he was back in town. Mica and Claire repaired the front door and locked up his house when they left. They cleaned the bullet casings littering the front drive but couldn't do anything about the tire marks in his yard. Mica added that Santino was without lasting injury, according to David, and he was resting at Ryan and Jenna's house under observation.

Claire had arranged a rental car for them at the airport.

"Claire texted me Zabner's address," he told Jess. "We can rent a hotel room nearby. Perhaps we'll call first thing tomorrow and then drop by his home."

"Which hotel?" Jess asked.

He slowed his pace so she could better walk beside him.

"A room with a bed," he said. Was she going to pick at unimportant details?

"I'm not staying in some fleabag motel."

"Fleabag motels take cash, and we need to keep you off the grid."

Jess grumbled. "The Ritz-Carlton has security."

Reece barked out an incredulous laugh.

"Okay," she conceded, failing to suppress a smile. "We don't have to stay in a five-star hotel, just not some filthy dump."

He stopped at the rental car line, five people back from the desk, and turned toward Jess. He restrained his temper as it simmered near the surface. In a low voice, he said, "I handle the covert part of the operation, and you handle the unveiling of medical facts. I won't tell you how to do your job, if you don't tell me how to do mine."

She blinked at him with pursed lips, once again unfazed by his intimidation tactics. It infuriated him even as he admired the trait.

"You certainly will have input on my part, and I will be receptive to your advice," she said, with the insinuation that he was to make the same offer.

He arched an eyebrow as his temper cooled. "Darling, every spy and thriller movie has the protagonist spending the night in some hole-in-the-wall motel. Holes are harder to trace."

"Yeah. And Hollywood never mentions the bed bugs—or lice."

"Jess—"

"Scabies."

"Jess—"

"Okay, anonymity is what you're concerned about, yes? Claire can *anonymously* rent a VRBO—vacation rental by owner. Everything is online, and most places have a lock box for the key."

"Vacation rental?" He didn't know whether to scream or laugh.

She glanced at the other people in the car rental line and lowered her voice to a harsh whisper. "If I'm going to get taken out by a hit squad, I'll at least have had a good night's rest."

"You have some strange priorities, sweetheart." Reece shook his head as he dialed Claire's number. No way they could get a VRBO on short notice but going through the motions would appease Jess.

"Hello?" Claire answered.

"I'm going to hand the phone to Jess, and the two of you can sort out where we'll be staying for the duration of our trip."

He passed the phone to Jess who walked a few paces away as he rubbed his temples. Vacation rental in the middle of a mission? What was this absurdity?

But the more he thought about it, the less he wanted to take Jess to a low-key motel. Nicer accommodations posed less of a security threat if rented through Claire and not in their names. He'd once stayed at a tropical resort in Antigua while on a job with Ryan. And to Jess's point about a good night's sleep, they did need to stay sharp.

It was nine o'clock at night by the time they drove the rental car to the vacation rental Claire had found and probably forked out a chunk of money to reserve so close to Christmas. Jess planned to reimburse Rider SI for the rental and pay for all of their tireless work.

She felt satisfaction in achieving the small accomplishment of obtaining nice, private accommodations. She understood Reece's view—how important was the quality of a room in the grand scheme of staying alive?

But if she was going to be on her top performance with Dr. Zabner and whatever new, insurmountable obstacles presented themselves, she needed a place to sleep that wouldn't have her questioning the hygiene.

Reece had abated his argument faster than usual. In exchange for his unspoken understanding, she'd held his hand as he drove the rented Honda Accord. But he'd been too preoccupied with security mode to notice. Guided by his phone's GPS, he watched for a tail with the mechanical fluidity of habit while his true thoughts seemed far away.

Maybe Jess's touch was silly under the circumstances. Reece was busy and focused. When she tried to pull her hand back, he squeezed his grip tighter and held her hand firmly in his even as he continued to focus on driving. The small gesture had heat zinging through her body.

When they arrived, he parked the Honda on the snowbanked curb. Together, with her luggage in Reece's grasp, they walked up the steps. Icy wind whipped through her hair and clawed her cheeks raw. He retrieved the key from the lockbox and let them inside the town home.

The warm air struck Jess's face and instantly soothed her chilled skin. Having spent time in Atlanta, she preferred the warmer weather. Yet something about returning to Chicago in the frigid cold of December felt like Christmas.

She glanced at Reece as he secured the door and set down her luggage. How long would the Luminous issue take to resolve? Was there a chance she could spend Christmas with her family—just stay in Chicago until the merry day arrived? Would Reece entertain the idea of joining her?

She turned away and began tugging off her coat. When had she become *that woman*—believing in fairy tales?

Reece stood behind her and helped her out of her coat. "I need to go pick up my equipment bag. I can get food while I'm out." His voice was low and close.

"I could use some comfort food," she admitted.

He gave her a brief squeeze and kissed the top of head.

She found a piece of paper and pen on the countertop. As she wrote down her order and the name of a takeout place she knew in the area, she heard Reece stepping outside and closing the door behind him. Apparently, he was in a hurry to get that equipment bag—of weapons, no doubt. If the urgency was real, why hadn't they stopped on the way to the townhome instead of him making a trip back out? Maybe he didn't want her knowing where the cache was stashed.

She scribbled faster and scurried to the door, not wanting to miss placing her order for comfort food. She needed to catch him before he reached the car.

From the other side of the door, she heard Reece's voice.

"Don't read me the riot act Claire. I just need Dr. Sullivan's address."

Jess stopped her hand from turning the doorknob. Reece's footfalls down the steps were followed by the engine starting.

Lori's address? He could have just asked her—unless he didn't want her to know where he was going.

REECE BLEW warm air into his hands. As he drove, he considered the stops he needed to make after he had his weapons bag—Lori Sullivan's place and takeout.

Reece parked at the self-storage unit off of Seventy-Ninth Street. He entered the building and punched the code on the electronic keypad of door B12. Stepping inside, he let the door close behind him. He retrieved one of the duffel bags and filled it with items he thought he'd need from the shelves—flashlight, MREs, thermal blanket, first aid kit, multi-tool, knife set, wire cutters, paracord, C4, detonators, two 9mm's with four clips, night vision goggles, binoculars, and five-hundred dollars cash. He pulled on a pair of thermal gloves made from a material thin enough to still pull a trigger. He pocketed one of the knives. He would use what he needed for this mission, replace the items later, and put the bag back in storage for the next operation.

After he left the self-storage center and was back in the rental car with the duffel in the passenger seat, he entered Dr. Sullivan's address from Claire into his phone app. The place had probably already been cleaned out by whoever had been after Lori Sullivan, but if even a minuscule chance existed that he could find something they could use to expose the pharmaceutical company and secure Jess's freedom, he had to try.

He couldn't shake the awful images of the car bomb. She'd been too close to danger. If she'd parked in the driveway instead of at the end of the driveway, the outcome would have been catastrophic—for both of them. And if she hadn't held him up to say thank-you, he would have been walking to the house and closest to the garage when the Porsche exploded.

When he pulled up to the brownstone, the street appeared quiescent. Only a few lights were on at this late hour. The exterior door light was off, so he thought he might be able to pick the lock and enter unseen.

He adjusted his wool coat and pulled on the hat he'd bought at the airport. After hopping out of the rental car, he walked quickly to Dr. Sullivan's front door. His hands were cold even through the gloves, and he struggled with the pick set. When the lock gave way, he let himself inside the dark room. Peering into the blackness, he looked for an alarm system as his eyes adjusted. He spotted the wall mount and shone his flashlight from his phone onto the rectangle.

Hmm. Already deactivated.

When his phone rang, he slipped in his earpiece. "Evening, Mica. To what do I owe the pleasure of your call?"

"Claire tells me you're going off script again."

"I had to come to Lori's place on the off chance that there might actually be something, anything, to make this investigation go in our favor."

"May I remind you that you have no backup?"

"The place is empty," Reece said. "Besides, someone has already been here, deactivated the alarm, and searched the place."

Based on dust patterns, someone had been here snooping before him—shelves with items moved created faint voids of dust from where they'd rested. Probably the same person or persons who'd deactivated the alarm.

He made rapid work of his inspection. "The search here was more covert than ransacking Jess's apartment or car-bombing Scott Gumpert."

"Let's talk through the sequence of events," Mica said. "Dr. Sullivan starts asking questions, which puts her on Poindexter Pharmaceutical's watch list. Except watching turns into to murder, or at least a car crash and early death. They need to ensure her secrets die with her, so they scour her home. But at some point before her death, they discover—or suspect—she sent information to Jess."

Reece picked up the conversation trail as he made his way to the bedroom and continued his search. "They phone a friend and distributor—Lautaro Fernandez—to cap the leak. Simultaneously, they know that Dr. Sullivan contacted Scott Gumpert, so now he's a liability, too."

"Why a car bomb?"

"Easy getaway for the killer. Messy but hard to trace."

"Find anything?" Mica asked.

He circled back to the living room. "The absence of a laptop or desktop. No flash drives or external storage devices. No notebooks for journaling."

"So, they wiped it clean?"

"Indeed. It seems we will be paying Zabner a visit tomorrow after all."

"Get out of there and be careful."

"Always." He clicked off the call, turned off the flashlight, and pocketed his phone and earpiece.

When he opened the front door to leave, an enormous figure filled the space. Immediately sensing the danger, Reece reached for his weapon.

Before Reece could aim and fire, the giant launched a reared back leg solidly into Reece's chest. His gun clattered to the floor.

He forcefully expelled air as the impact sent him sprawling backward and into the couch in the living room.

The enormous attacker entered the brownstone. He was unnaturally tall with square shoulders and an oversized head, making him look like Frankenstein's monster's silhouette as he stalked toward Reece in the dark.

Reece struggled to get to his feet as his rubbery legs refused to fully cooperate. Gasping for air, his chest throbbed as if it had been hit with a battering ram, and his back reminded him of the car bomb earlier. Pain blurred his vision.

The largest foot Reece had ever seen, encased in a massive work boot, came at him again.

He clicked open the pocketknife he'd retrieved while writhing on the floor and buried it into the man's calf. The leg continued its trajectory into Reece's side even as the beastly monster howled.

Reece tried to duck and roll with the blow, but he'd had to expose his side to succeed in the knife counterattack. Once again, pain burst through his body, which then refused to cooperate with a hasty retreat. If he could skirt around the giant, he could retrieve his gun by the front door, but he doubted he'd be fast enough in his current condition. Too bad he didn't still have that Taser.

As the man approached, his new limp only added to the intimidation rather than making him appear weakened.

When he was directly over Reece, he didn't attempt to kick again—either because of the pain of the knife wound or the living room furniture in the way.

Reece launched with an uppercut all the way to the man's face. He felt as if he was leaping for a ten-foot lay-up. Oof. Nothing but rim. The man's jaw must have been made of steel because jarring pain reverberated from Reece's elbow all the way to his shoulder.

The monster grunted and stumbled back a step but not before lashing out a hand that wrapped around Reece's neck. The giant's massive grip squeezed, cutting off both air flow and blood flow.

With both hands, Reece clutched the tree trunk of an arm restraining him, digging in with his fingers to try to loosen the vise grip by injuring the tendons. The man didn't budge, and Reece knew he had only seconds left to live.

Miserably, he realized he'd failed Jess. Without him, she would be even more vulnerable to an attack. His solo mission would be her downfall. He hated to think he had no time left in this world with her.

17

*J*ess picked up the 9 mm on the floor and fired. The bull of a man strangling Reece let loose his grip, and Reece crashed to the floor, gasping for air.

Damn, these things were loud. If she ever owned a gun, she'd put a silencer on it.

Keeping the weapon trained on the attacker, she said, "I'm going to go ahead and point out that my Minotaur analogy was accurate. That thing on the floor is more bull than man."

Snark again. She was at a loss for what else to do. The physician in her wanted to rush to Reece and make sure he was okay, but she couldn't risk this thing getting up off the floor and reengaging Reece in a gladiator battle to the death in Lori's living room.

Her love for Reece caused an unfamiliar rage that channeled energy into the shaking hand holding the gun, demanding her to put another bullet in the man who had attempted to snuff out Reece's life.

Painstakingly, Reece pushed to his feet. He grimaced as he ambled over to her. "We need to leave, now."

He took the gun from her but slung an arm around her shoulder and let her take some of his weight. She helped him to the rental car as they left the Minotaur bleeding on Lori's living room carpet.

"How did you get here?" he asked.

"Rideshare. I know I had to use my phone, but you left me no choice."

He nodded as he handed her the keys and holstered his weapon.

She helped him into the passenger seat before rushing around to the driver's side and starting the car. She jetted out of the neighborhood as fast as she could while still staying mindful of the icy pavement.

They rode in silence as her emotions warred with each other. She was furious at him for attempting this alone and worried about how serious his injuries might be. Even more, it scared her that he wasn't chastising her right now for coming to his rescue.

When they arrived back at the townhome, she helped him out of the car and unlocked the front door with the key. As she led him toward the living room couch, she swung a foot out and closed the front door.

"I'm going to see if I can find a first aid kit and get a shit ton of ice. And then we'll talk."

"There's a first aid kit in the go bag in the trunk." He started to stand.

"Stay. I'll get it."

She went back to the car, opened the trunk, and lifted the gargantuan black duffel bag. "Damn." She grunted. "And he gives me a hard time about my luggage."

After retrieving the huge bag and lugging it inside, she bolted and locked the door. While she fixed a glass of water with eight hundred milligrams of ibuprofen, Reece retrieved the first aid kit out of the bag and set it on the coffee table. She inspected the contents—adequate for blisters and second-degree burns but not so much for internal organ injuries. She fetched three bags of ice as he gulped down the medication without question and finished off the glass of water.

"Where do these need to go, and do I need more?" She gestured to the ice.

"I was kicked here and here and strangled here."

She inspected the area where he was kicked and didn't find any broken ribs, but the tenderness suggested she would need to keep an eye on him to make sure the bleeding was localized and not involving internal organs. If it had been anyone else but him, she would've bullied him into going to an emergency room for imaging. But she knew Reece wouldn't comply. After her inspection, she applied ice to all of the injured areas as Reece lay back on the couch. She took off his boots so he could prop up his feet.

"I'm so pissed at you right now I can't even see straight," Jess said in a low, searing voice.

"I know." His tone was one of defeat and remorse.

"I can't believe you tried to do that alone, knowing what we're up against."

"I shouldn't have."

"I can't—" She took a shaky breath. "I understand that you want to protect me, and you want to do as much of this as you can without putting me in danger, but if you die, I'm finished." Emotionally and physically, but she didn't elaborate further. "We have to work as a team. Promise me we're going to see this through to the end together."

"I promise."

His anguished expression had her wanting to crawl up on the

couch beside him. But she needed to let him rest. They still had another escapade to execute during their time in Chicago.

"You'd better not try something like this again, and if you do, you pick up the food *before* you go getting your ass kicked by a Minotaur."

He didn't laugh or fire back with his own quip. Not a good sign in regard to his injuries.

She sighed. "I saw some cans in the pantry. I'll go make us some soup."

JESS WOKE beside Reece in bed as the sun streamed through the window. After the beating he'd taken last night, she'd helped him to the master bedroom, and they'd gotten seven hours of solid sleep.

She carefully moved the sheets down to look at his bare back. Grimacing at the appearance of the bruises, she resisted the urge to lower her lips to the battered surface and kiss away his poor injuries. She didn't want to wake him.

He was still dressed in jeans from the waist down, and since she hadn't thought to buy pajamas at the airport, she'd slept in her cotton stretch pants and oversized sweater.

Of their own volition, her fingers moved along the muscles of his back. He was fortunate not to have any broken ribs after being tossed around like a rag doll from both the bomb and the Minotaur's brutality.

Reece rolled over, startling her as he pulled her into his arms. "Your touch is a nice way to wake up."

She smiled. "I can make a breakfast run. You probably need more ibuprofen too."

"Are you hungry now?" His warm breath caressed her neck as

he buried his face in her hair.

She froze. Intimacy with Reece was the one thing that could always stave off her desires for food.

She swallowed. "Not right now."

His hands moved down her sweater before venturing beneath the material.

She sucked in a breath.

He pressed his lips to her neck. "Are my hands too cold?"

"No." His hands felt warm like his lips. The calluses moved over her skin, leaving a trail of sizzling heat in their wake. His mustache skimmed her neck with every kiss.

How could every time together be this intoxicating? How was he so freely giving of his passion in bed but afraid to commit to sharing a life together?

Jess couldn't dwell on that. She would take whatever he was willing to give in this moment. But she would give too. He would know that their time spent together would never be one-sided.

They discarded their clothing and lay naked side by side. She kissed him on the lips, her tongue exploring and taking the moment deeper into the fiery well of emotion. When she slid her hands around his broad chest, he groaned into the kiss.

The power she wielded over him excited her further and caused her to surrender more of herself to him.

Although he hadn't complained about them, she thought of his injuries. "I don't want to hurt you," she said.

He grinned as he rolled so that she was on top of him. "Then I guess you'd better take the reins."

They took their fill of each other until Jess floated on a cloud of release to the sound of Reece's own pleasure as he cried out her name.

"Jessica."

·   ·   ·

JESS LAY SPENT, looking up at the ceiling as Reece breathed heavily beside her. All of this time with him was weakening the fortification she'd built to seal off the emotions she harbored for him. She was going to hurt all over again when this ended… badly. As it had done before.

She remembered the terrible day of their last fight. She'd woken, snuggled up beside Reece's firm, warm body. Her affection for Reece had flooded her emotions. She'd wanted to tell him how she felt with words, but it'd seemed a delicate matter—as if she stared at a rickety bridge strung across a gorge. On the other side was a union with Reece—she hadn't been pining for marriage but at least hoped for a more permanent relationship than what they had. She would have to navigate that bridge to reach her ideal relationship, and one misstep on the wrong board, one disproportionate amount of weight or pressure in the wrong spot, and she would free-fall away from her desires.

Would saying those three little words cause a plank on the bridge to snap? She hadn't been sure, so she'd avoided it, doing everything she could to show him instead of tell him. She wouldn't be the first to say it, even if the phrase was true.

"Hello, beautiful," Reece had said.

She recalled the way the afternoon sun through the window had cast a golden glow on his skin. She'd smiled as she summoned the courage to make her request. She hadn't touched him, didn't stroke his chest or purr against him. She wouldn't try to seduce him into giving her the answer she wanted.

"I fly up to Chicago tomorrow for a few shifts. Since you're not on an assignment right now, I thought you might join me."

He must have sensed something in her voice because he'd raised a speculative eyebrow rather than agreeing to come with her.

She continued, "I was hoping you might have dinner with my

family."

And there it was—invitation cast. The lump in her throat hardened as the temperature in the bedroom plummeted.

"I'll think about it." His voice was cautious as he rolled out of bed and began to dress, emotionally closing himself off to her —again.

She pulled the covers up around her as she leaned against the headboard. Anger and hurt battled inside her. She willed herself not to say anything crass. Lashing out would only make the situation worse. But keeping her mouth shut wasn't a strength she possessed.

"It's one dinner," she said flatly. "It would probably be the least dangerous thing you do all month." Meeting the parents was a next step in their relationship they hadn't yet taken. The symbolic step toward commitment was small but significant.

He pulled on his T-shirt without making eye contact. "I said I'll think about. I have to make sure nothing new comes up at work. It can be unpredictable."

Her face grew hot. *Oh, that tone*, she seethed. She hated the way a man could imply a woman was overreacting by the patronizing tone in his voice, even as he knew his body language was cold and demeaning.

"I know your work is unpredictable. I'm asking for one dinner." Asking and not begging. She would never beg.

"I'll think about it," he repeated. When he was angry or upset, his sentences became shorter, less loquacious.

The irritation in his voice felt like a slap in the face—as if she was the one being unreasonable.

"It's just dinner," she snapped.

He glared at her as he shoved his foot into his last boot and straightened. "Then why are you so bent out of shape about it?"

She remained unmoving on the bed. "I want you to meet my

parents. Why is it hard for you to agree to that?"

"I didn't say no."

"You might as well have."

"You're overreacting, Jess."

"You haven't even begun to see me overreact." She bit out the words. "Why are you pushing me away?"

"My life is danger. Maybe I don't want you to be a part of that danger."

"That's not a good reason. I've been a part of your life for a few years. You wait to worry about my safety until a visit to my parents is involved? And what about all of the other Rider members who have relationships?"

He snatched his keys off the dresser. "I'm going to get breakfast. I'll see you when I get back."

"No. You won't." She threw off the covers and began to get dressed.

"What in the hell is that supposed to mean?"

"I will spell it out for you. You are being an ass. I won't be here when you get back. If you want to fix this, you have my number."

"Are you giving me an ultimatum?"

"No. An opportunity. One I'm not sure you deserve." She shrugged on her jacket as he got nose to nose with her.

"An opportunity? To what? Grovel at the feet of her highness to meet the parents? Forget it. I hope you are gone when I come back, and don't expect a call from me. We're finished."

Feeling raw and gutted, she'd stormed around him and out the bedroom door. "Damn right we are."

REECE KISSED his way down Jess's bare shoulder, ready for round two. He wanted to tell her how he felt but showing her seemed richer and more authentic. Making love seemed like a deeper form of emotion than uttering the words. But he knew she needed to hear the words too.

He would live wherever she wanted—Chicago, Atlanta, or Timbuktu. Obviously, he would keep his home in Atlanta, since several rooms in the house had been finished with her in mind. In fact, if she wanted to continue to alternate cities, he'd be supportive of that as well. They had time to discuss and work through the details.

He wove his fingers through her long, silky hair as he pressed his body closer to her. "Jess—"

His phone rang. "*Sonofa*—" Sighing, he reached for it and seeing it was Claire, put her on speakerphone.

"Good morning, Claire. What news have you to bequeath us?" He let his irritation fade. He knew she was working double time on this case, and he and Jess needed to continue their investigation.

"Zabner isn't answering my calls. Maybe he doesn't answer unknown callers. I think you'll have to just drop by his place. According to his calendar app, he's off today."

Reece sat up in bed and checked the clock: Saturday, eight a.m. "Next stop, Dr. Zabner's home."

"I'll text you the address."

"Thank you, Claire."

Claire disconnected the call.

He rolled out of bed and stood.

"Breakfast first," Jess corrected him with a smile.

When he shook his head, she gently slapped his exposed bottom. "You know the ICU team calls me the ragin' Asian when I get hangry."

He planted a kiss on her lips before dressing. "I'll take care of you... and your stomach."

18

Mica steeled herself as she entered the visitation room of the US Penitentiary in Atlanta. Lucius Titan sat in a wheelchair wearing the same khaki jumper he'd worn on her last visit. Trim hair framed a lightly tanned face. He didn't appear to be suffering one ounce as he served his time.

But she knew this was part of his facade. He was physically handicapped and locked behind bars. He was making the most of a miserable situation, though his predicament was entirely of his own making and probably better than he deserved.

He gave Mica a smile, warm but tired around the edges. His dark eyes weren't nearly as calculating as they usually were. Was he breaking under the strain of captivity?

"Lucius." She took a seat across from him at the table.

The guard overseeing their interaction stood a respectful distance out of earshot.

"Always a pleasure to see you, Mica," Lucius purred.

"You seem to be keeping close tabs on my company and my people."

He locked gazes with her. "Mostly just you."

She suppressed the urge to shudder. She did not want to be this sociopath's object of affection. Yet if he had information of value to her team, she could suffer through an interaction with him.

"You have information on Lautaro?" she asked.

"I do."

She'd observed that Lucius had no characteristic quirks. He didn't fidget or shift his weight. He always seemed utterly calm. He was the crocodile beneath tranquil water. He was the saw-scaled viper coiled and still in a rock crevice until it struck with deadly venom.

He folded his hands on the table. "Lautaro, as I'm sure you're already aware, made his beginnings in drug labs in Argentina. He distributes to America but only recently has been trying to be more involved in direct sales. A few years ago, he tried to expand to Europe. Of course, with Maxine Rider's help, Vladimir Pronin crushed that expansion."

Mica hadn't been part of those events, but she was familiar with how things had unfolded. She had also discussed the events with one of Rider SI's part-time employees, Dorian, who had told her everything he knew about Lautaro from his previous work with Rider and elsewhere, along with everything he'd learned during his last few days of investigation.

Mica said, "Lautaro's growing expansion into the US is funded by this new narcotic on the streets—Luminous."

"Precisely right."

"And Luminous is none other than trihydrodone—a prescription narcotic currently in drug trials through a pharmaceutical company out of Chicago." She stated the conjecture as fact even though they hadn't proven it yet.

Lucius arched a dark eyebrow. "Very impressive."

So, Lori Sullivan's theory was correct. Mica appreciated knowing the truth, but they would still need the evidence. Ryan had checked with a source, Cuban mafia leader Ernesto Busta, who knew of the drug but not its owner. He could only assert that Luminous wasn't made by Lautaro's organization.

"We had to work fast, since Lautaro is trying to stop us from proving it," Mica said, not willing to betray how Lucius's praise both stroked her pride and repulsed her.

"He's not the one you need to worry about."

Mica's teeth grated against each other. She waited as Lucius drew out the suspense.

"Poindexter Pharmaceutical hired the Shoup Group to play middleman between them and Lautaro. As well as protect their financial interests."

The Shoup Group. Mica had heard of them—another dark ex-military organization who placed monetary gain above morality. Eliminating—or at least marginalizing—Titan Enterprises had created a void. The Shoup Group had expanded to fill it.

Lucius pursed his lips. "I see you're appropriately concerned. You've heard of them, so you also know what they're capable of."

"Everything you were."

"Exactly."

"They killed Dr. Sullivan because she threatened to expose them." She spoke the words as a statement of fact but still hoped Lucius would verify or deny it.

"Likely, I'm sure. But I can't confirm that for you based on my sources."

The Shoup Group's involvement explained the bizarre differences in attack strategies. Lautaro sent brutes after Dr. Ong and gunslingers after Reece, while the Shoup Group probably planted Gumpert's car bomb and killed Lori Sullivan in a car crash—

though Mica didn't know if the latter was intentional or inadvertent.

Her mind started to churn with ideas of how the Rider team would need to up their game if they were going to face off against the Shoup Group. There would be no bargaining. If they'd been paid to eliminate threats to Poindexter like Jessica Ong and now Reece, they would be unrelenting in the pursuit of their goal. The only way to resolve the situation was by exposing the drug company. Once the damage was done, the Shoup Group would have failed in their mission to silence Dr. Ong and would have no further role. Mica hoped.

"Who is orchestrating this at Poindexter Pharmaceutical?"

Lucius rolled his shoulders. "Supposedly one of their research directors and a few of his minions. They aren't a threat to you."

"Maybe not, but I'm going to make sure whoever is responsible for starting this supply chain of a dangerous drug onto the streets is apprehended by authorities."

"What a knight in shining armor you are!" He smiled a brilliant set of white teeth.

Unable to tell if he was mocking her, she ignored the comment. "Why warn me about the Shoup Group? Telling me helps me better prepare. You could keep quiet and let Shoup win this round. It would be a big loss for Rider SI."

He tilted his head to one side. "I could tell you I've grown fond of you and your rag-tag team of philanthropic bleeding hearts, but you're more likely to believe that I subscribe to the ancient proverb, '*The enemy of my enemy is my friend.*'"

Mica grunted. Yes, she could believe that.

"I won't always be trapped in this cage. When I'm out, I don't want to discover Shoup has gobbled up all of the business." He grinned, a little devious but still with a hint of fatigue eroding the edges.

"We'll certainly do our best to slow their progress, though for the good of our clients and not for your benefit." Although she'd come to him for information, she needed to maintain clear boundaries with a man like him.

"I expected as much."

Mica stood, gave Lucius a rare soft smile, and nodded her head in the closest thing she would ever give him to a thank-you. She needed get back to work and dig deeper into their new rival—the Shoup Group.

JESS PARKED the rented Accord on the curb outside Zabner's house at nine thirty a.m. Snow blanketed the cozy neighborhood, coating the rooftops of the two-story homes along the block. Most of the houses had Christmas lights draped over windows and bushes. The researcher's house was one of the few without decorations. Jess wondered why. Different religion? Was he a workaholic with no time for frivolities? Was he too busy selling trihydrodone to drug dealers?

What if Lori had approached him for help and he'd been the one to expose her investigation and get her killed?

One brave soul walked his black Lab down the sidewalk, but everyone else remained indoors and out of the cold. Based on the heavy clouds, Jess wondered if more snow was expected that afternoon.

When she realized Reece was already out of the car, she scurried to keep up with his long strides to Zabner's front door. No lights shone from inside the house. Reece knocked briskly and rang the bell. Although his gun was holstered, she knew he could draw it in one second flat.

Only silence greeted them. Jess strained for even the sound of footsteps on stairs but heard nothing.

"I'll be back." Reece began peering into windows as he circled the house.

Jess, hands buried in her jacket pockets, bounced lightly on her toes to help keep warm. She was tempted to kick in the door just to get inside to warmth—not that she actually believed she was capable of kicking down a door.

Reece appeared from around the side of the house. "Follow me around back."

"See anything?" She followed.

"No. But the backyard has foliage, so we're less likely to be seen when we go inside the house."

He led her through a waist-high wooden gate and re-latched it after they were in the backyard under cover of pine trees over a small rectangle of snow-covered grass. He glanced around.

"How are we getting inside?" she asked.

He answered her by pulling out a lockpick. He tugged a glove off, and it dangled between his teeth as he set to work. Judging by his grimace, yesterday's injuries were causing him pain.

"Shit. We're breaking and entering." Jess glanced around to see the privacy trees hiding the yard. Nevertheless, spying neighbors with nothing better to do than stare out their windows on a cold day might be able to spot their activity.

She wondered if this was how he'd entered Lori's place last night. He'd already been inside her brownstone by the time Jess arrived, since she'd wasted precious time pacing and debating if she should go after him at all. She shuddered as she remembered the violent kick of the gun and smell of gunpowder—a mix of metallic charred meat with a touch of sulfur. Without hesitation, she'd shot a man. It hadn't been fatal, and she didn't feel an ounce of remorse. It had been him or Reece.

"Keep your hands to yourself when we're inside," he told her.

"Yeah, I figured as much. Is there an alarm system?"

"I looked. No keypad."

"What about bombs?"

"Let's not take his car for a test drive."

Jess followed Reece inside, bracing herself for the sound of a home alarm. Instead, a foul odor accosted her nose.

She put her hand to her face. "Holy crap! What died in here?" But as soon as she spoke the words, she suspected she knew the answer.

She wanted to turn around and march back out into the cold, but they'd come in search of explanations and couldn't leave without them. Except she suspected they might leave with some unanswered questions and some entirely new ones.

Reece kept silent as he stalked though the house, gun in hand.

She wanted to tell him no one was suffering this stench just to lie in wait and attack, but she kept quiet to let him do his security thing.

After they'd circled the kitchen, living room, and dining room —leaving the tidy space undisturbed, they advanced toward the stairs. The source of the smell clearly originated upstairs.

"Bah. I could never be a coroner. Decomposed flesh is awful."

"None of your patients smell this bad?"

"This is worse than a GI bleed. It may be equivalent to a patient I once had who came in with septic shock from a gangrene leg half covered in maggots."

"That is some graphic imagery I could do without," he said.

When they reached the master bedroom, a body lay on the bed. Jess hung back at the entrance, her sleeve over her mouth and nose for all the good it did. She didn't need to get up close and personal to know the man was beyond help. A small pit of guilt formed at having wondered if Zabner had played a role in Lori's death—now knowing he was also dead. Poindexter's cover-up seemed to know no bounds.

Reece advanced inside slowly, inspecting the corpse and the room without touching anything.

"Please tell me you're not going to check for a pulse."

"One does not need a medical degree to know Dr. Zabner has gone with God."

"Can we go now?"

"One moment."

Jess backed away and waited by the stairs while Reece checked the other room. In the silence, she replayed the shooting last night in her mind. She'd only been target shooting with Reece twice, at his insistence. Her aim hadn't been very good, the weapons were loud, and the kick was jarring. Yet when she'd shot the Minotaur, she hadn't hesitated. Reece's life had been in danger.

Then, they'd left the man bleeding on the floor. The bullet entry point didn't lead to any vital organs, but it could still have ricocheted off the pelvic bone and into the abdomen or an artery. And if he didn't get proper medical treatment, he could still die of an infection. The thought that she could be responsible for killing someone sickened her. And yet, if her actions meant saving Reece, she would do it all again.

When they went back downstairs, Reece confiscated keys and a key card from a coat hanging by the door.

They left the house out the back door and got back inside their rental car.

"I feel like we should have covered him up and said last rites or something, but instead we're robbing the grave—taking his key card."

Reece blinked at her as he pulled away from the curb.

"I get it. I get it." She extended her hands in front of the car's air vents to thaw her fingers. "We need to leave no evidence we were there. Still makes me sad."

She'd seen Reece keep his gloves on to avoid touching anything with his bare hands.

She added, "I didn't get close enough to tell, but I'm sure Zabner didn't just happen to die of natural causes at the same time Lori died in a motor vehicle crash."

"Single shot bullet wound to his head. Probably never woke with the intruder in his house. Very professional."

"No forced entry," Jess added. She frowned. "Isn't this a different mode of operation from the men who came after us? Is that normal?"

"Different city, different personnel perhaps. But I will concede that the level of professionalism is worrisome."

"What were you looking for in the bedroom?"

"Laptop. There was no computer in his downstairs rooms or in the bedroom turned office space upstairs. And no laptop anywhere. I would have liked to get his laptop into Claire's hands, but it seems the company has covered its tracks once again."

"Not the badge though. I saw you snag that."

"Yes, they overlooked his office access badge. And I took his keys in case they open something at his workplace."

"Seems we have another B and E in our future. Is it breaking and entering if we have a badge? Maybe it's S and E. Sneaking and entering."

Reece pursed his lips, and Jess realized he wasn't happy with the idea of entering the research facility. Why? It was the next logical step if they were going to get a sample of trihydrodone. He'd obviously taken the badge and keys thinking the same thing. Perhaps the bad guys would draw the same conclusion. They seemed to be one step ahead of Reece and Jess this entire time.

Was Reece worried it could be a trap?

19

Reece paced the small living room of their rental home as the video conference began. He rolled his shoulders and stretched his sides, noting the aches and pains from getting his butt kicked yesterday in the surprise attack at Lori's place.

Mica and Claire came into view—Claire from the office and Mica from home, judging by their clothing and the backgrounds familiar to him. He had texted them that they needed an emergency planning meeting.

"What's the update?" Mica asked.

Reece placed his hands on the back of the couch where Jess sat. He leaned forward, facing the computer screen. "Zabner is dead. Murdered."

"*Sh... sugar.*" Mica ran a hand through her blonde hair. "Another bomb?"

Reece shook his head. "Bullet to his head in his sleep. Professional."

"And you have additional obstacles," Mica said. "Poindexter Pharmaceutical hired the Shoup Group."

"Dammit to hell." He instantly regretted his outburst, which indicated the severity of their situation to Jess. "That explains the professional hit at the researcher's home."

"What's the Shoup Group?" Jess asked.

"Private security. The bad kind—like what Lucius's team used to be. Or probably still is," Reece answered.

"And they're based out of Chicago," Mica added.

"Which means we need to act now," he said.

"Why the rush?" Jess asked.

Claire said, "They have the resources to figure out you're in Chicago."

Reece thought about his fight at Lori Sullivan's house. The giant probably worked for the Shoup Group and reported to them after last night's fight, which meant the ruthless organization already knew Reece was not only in Chicago but looking for answers. Alternatively, they could have posted the assassin there knowing he and Jess had come to Chicago and hoping to catch them investigating. Either way, it was bad news all around.

"But not our specific location. It's not rented under our name," Jess said.

Reece came around the couch and sat beside Jess. "It's likely they know we're in Chicago from the plane flight and rental car." There had been no getting around those being in their names since a driver's license were required for both. "And my debacle last night," he added bitterly. "They'll suspect we're searching for the truth, and they'll work harder to cover their tracks. That will make our goal of linking the trial drug with the street drug more difficult."

It couldn't be any more difficult, he thought.

They'd struck out three times now—Gumpert, Sullivan, and Zabner.

"So we go now," Jess said. "It's a Saturday. We use Zabner's badge to get into the building." Her voice rose with urgency. She turned from Reece to Claire. "Can you tell us where Zabner's office is located within Poindexter Pharmaceutical or where some of the drug might be stored within their complex?"

"First of all," Reece interjected, wagging a finger at her, "there is no *we* in a mission like this. You're an unqualified civilian. And if we encounter any of Shoup's men, they will shoot to kill." He hadn't forgotten his promise of teamwork last night, but that discussion hadn't included going into a secure building owned by a company who'd hired ruthless, unscrupulous mercenaries.

Jess pinched the bridge of her nose as she stood up from the couch. "Okay," she began calmly, "I'm going to take your egotistical comments and chalk them up to a poor choice of words as a reflection of how your emotional entanglement with me has you so worried you can't think straight. I'm also going to remind you that I saved you last night by shooting someone in the ass. And to be clear"—she poked a finger into his chest—"I am *the most* qualified person to find the information we need from inside that lab. Seriously," she huffed, turning back to look at Mica and Claire on the screen, "can I get someone from your team who has a level head?" She smirked and jerked her thumb in Reece's direction. "I don't want this guy screwing up *my* mission."

Mica and Claire glanced nervously in Reece's direction as if he might detonate.

Reece shoved to his feet, ready for an argument with Jess. How dare she be so glib about the danger?

The look behind her facade of courage silenced him. The rest of her body language was plain as day for him to see—pinched brow, hands gripped tightly together, and lost brown eyes. He turned away and ran a ragged hand through his hair, forcing himself to be calm. Jess was as terrified for her own safety as he was.

She was so damn tough that she knew how to put on a brave face. The realization had him second-guessing their other times together. What about all of their other arguments? She could cut him down as easily as she built him up. Had those fights been indicative of her deeper insecurities?

And what did it say about him as a partner if he made her feel too insecure to express herself normally and if he didn't offer reassurance to ease her fears?

Damn worthless, that was what it made him.

Claire cleared her throat, "We sent Santino and Ryan to the airport this morning, but they won't reach you in time between flight delays and cancellations."

"Reece?" Mica said after a long stretch of silence.

He held up a hand to the computer. "Dammit. Okay. Jess is right. I need her." He needed her in every sense of the word—friend, lover, companion, and partner for this mission. He sat back down on the couch, facing the woman he loved. "I need your help when we breach the lab." Because she looked like she was bracing for a stipulation, he added, "I can't do this without you."

She swallowed and blinked away tears. He tried to remember if she'd ever cried in front of him before. Had he never given her the security to cry in front of him? What kind of asshole was he?

He could fix this. He would fix this.

He placed his hands on her shoulders. "I will protect you. We'll infiltrate, confiscate the files or a sample or whatever we need, and get out. I'll keep you safe."

WHILE CLAIRE LOOKED UP schematic information on Poindexter Pharmaceutical's Chicago facility, Jess called her brother. Jay. She thought about how it was Saturday afternoon. The weather was too cold for her nieces to have outside activities, so they were probably playing indoors. Perhaps at the trampoline park, the YMCA, or the arcades. Jay usually tried to spend Saturdays exhausting them while only succeeding in exhausting himself.

To her relief, he answered the phone on the third ring. "Hello?"

"Hi, Jay."

"Jess? Where are you calling from? This isn't your mobile number."

"I'm spending some time with a friend. How are the girls?"

"They're good. I need a bottle of aspirin after two hours spent in the line to see the mall Santa. At least he had a real beard. That was cool. And we got some great photographs of the girls in his lap, minor bribing with chocolate required. We scored real smiles this time rather than stranger-anxiety-induced crying."

"You'll have to send me the pictures." But as soon as the words were out of her mouth, she realized she couldn't turn on her phone to look at them. When this ordeal concluded, she'd appreciate them. She'd never felt an urge to have children of her own, but she immensely enjoyed being the fun, quirky aunt at vacations and holidays.

"Yeah. I'll share them with you." Jay continued, "You'll be at Mom's for Christmas? I know I already asked, but she's worried."

"I'm looking forward to it." She wasn't sure if she was looking forward more to surviving to be able to go to Christmas or Christmas itself. "Listen, Jay. I think I have a story for you. Do you remember the research project I was trying to get published about the street narcotic?" After a stretch of silence, Jess said, "Never mind. It's fine. I don't remember all of your articles either."

"I'm sorry."

"No, really, I'm not offended. Anyway, this illegal street drug is killing people. I realize that part is not exactly a news flash, but there may be a connection with it and another drug—a trial drug manufactured by a pharmaceutical company. I don't have enough information yet, so I can't give you all the details. But I'm working to prove it."

"I'll listen to anything you want to pitch," he spoke cautiously. "But ultimately the topics are up to my editor."

"I know. I'm not trying to get you to commit to anything. I just want to give you a heads-up so that if I send you information, you'll know why I did it."

"That's cryptic. All you have to do is call me when you press the send button and explain."

Jess thought about Lori and the information she'd sent. Jay would be her backup plan. "There's a possibility I might not get that chance. What I'm looking into is a scandal and a conspiracy theory. If I'm wrong, then I'll just be arrested for trespassing on private property. If I'm right—and judging by the fact that I've been shot at and three people are dead, I'm right—then getting the proof I need to substantiate my accusation could be dangerous."

"Shot at?" Jay's tone sharpened. "People are dead? You need to give me more information. What are you talking about?"

"I'm talking about a conspiracy and a scandal," she repeated. "I'll send you more information as soon as I have it."

"You can't leave me hanging like this. You can't insinuate your life is in danger and then end the conversation."

"If I'm right, I will send you all the information, and you'll understand." Trying to explain the circumstances in detail to her brother would only result in him having more questions. She didn't have time for a two-hour discussion that would inevitably lead to an argument. She didn't need another man telling her to sit this one out. Or he would try to tell her how to handle it differently, even though he didn't understand the situation. Jess intended to see this through for Lori and all the victims of trihydrodone and Luminous.

If she gave Jay the information now, he'd start digging and paint a bull's-eye on his back before the Rider team could put protection on him. But if she did end up sending him information that proved her theory, she didn't want to pull a Lori Sullivan—she didn't want to plop dangerous information in his lap with zero explanation.

With that thought, she decided she would give Jay more information, but she would type it in a cohesive and comprehensive format. In this way, he wouldn't be in the dark waiting for her call, and she wouldn't be left talking with an angry frustrated brother who was questioning her actions and endeavors.

"I'll call you tomorrow." She didn't add, *If I can.*

JESS LEANED FORWARD and focused intently as Claire explained the layout of the research compound. Reece had returned to pacing behind her, which was a mercy because she'd nearly broken down and cried in his arms during their last video conference. Such an emotional display would have been counterproductive.

"The building is a three-story stand-alone structure. It's U-shaped with a little park-type area where employees can take breaks—not that anyone would be putting that to good use, since it's fifteen degrees outside in Chicago right now." Claire utilized the share screen option as she showed pictures of the building.

Most of the research center was made of glass, which in the photo—clearly pirated off their website—reflected a blue sky and lush green grass. Jess suspected it would look gray and foreboding under a winter sky, though perhaps she was projecting her own mood.

Claire continued, "The first floor has the main entrance with a security desk positioned to see incoming visitors. On either side, badge-access employee-only doors lead to employee parking. Elevators are located behind the security desk."

"Do we have to pass behind the security desk?" Jess asked. "Is it manned around the clock?"

"Stairs?" Reece asked.

"Exactly," Claire said. "Since security is likely twenty-four seven at a place like this—which I would confirm if I'd had time—you will bypass them by taking the stairs, which are located on either side near the employee entrances."

"We still need a distraction," Reece said.

"Right," Mica agreed. "We don't know if the key card access makes a beep that alerts security or if the stairwell door will be noisy. We can't assume gaining access—even with an employee badge—will be seamless."

"Special delivery?" Reece asked.

"Yes," Mica agreed.

Jess turned to look at Reece. "What does that mean? Special delivery?"

"A distraction. We hire a delivery, like a gift basket, to be sent to the front desk. The distraction of a random delivery for someone not at the office will be timed with our entry."

"Okay. Then what?"

Claire continued, "The lab is on the second floor with the research offices. The third floor is all administration, finances, and marketing."

"So we go to the second floor," Jess said. "Then what?"

"That's where you come in." Reece leaned over the sofa,

placing his hands on her shoulders. The warm, gentle touch gave her reassurance. "You snoop around and see where a sample might be. Maybe we steal other information while we're at it."

"Okay," Jess said. "And then out the same way we came in?"

"Yes," Mica said.

Jess thought about the laws they'd be breaking. In contrast, if they didn't expose the company, they couldn't shut down the trial and the illegal distribution.

People were dying.

Reece squeezed Jess's shoulders before releasing her. She knew this little planning session didn't account for the myriad of things that could go wrong—that *would* go wrong given their success rate so far with literal dead ends, Gumpert and Zabner. She understood they may need to improvise, but she trusted Reece in this aspect.

He had looked her in the eye and sworn he'd protect her. She believed him.

Something more lurked behind his pledge of allegiance, but she couldn't discern what it was and feared hoping for too much. They needed to survive the night first and discuss their feelings and future relationship later.

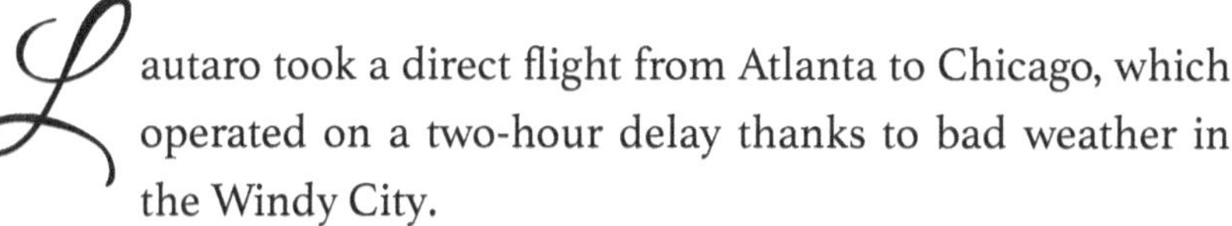autaro took a direct flight from Atlanta to Chicago, which operated on a two-hour delay thanks to bad weather in the Windy City.

Pedazo de mierda North American weather.

If he'd stayed in South America this winter, he could be lapping up the sun on a topless beach, not deboarding a plane in a frozen hellhole. He tightened his coat more firmly around his neck. Why would anyone want to live in a place this cold? City-dwelling rats who scurried from apartments to work and back, that was who.

And yet how critical of these people could he be? The miserable masses were the ones who paid for his drugs. His lifestyle was funded by their search for escape—escape from the cold, the loneliness, the stress, the boredom, the unfaithful spouses, the degenerate kids, the gluttonous bosses, the over-bearing families, the depression, and the anxiety.

Drugs had been the leading cause of arrest in the US in the last ten years. And the laughable irony was that most of those arrests were for petty possession. North American idiots spent fifty billion dollars a year—*todos los años!*—for a war on drugs they were losing.

Lautaro pushed through the crowd to get to the limousine his assistant had arranged for him.

Policymakers needed only to look in the faces of their American constituents to know the solution to the drug crisis. Or read people's cry for help in social media postings. To cure the country's drug problem, they needed to cure the country's mental health problem. They didn't need a war on drugs but a war on mental illness.

Of course, Lautaro certainly wasn't going to enlighten the US government or the public. He planned to keep the people in constant supply of whatever their drug of preference was—cocaine, ecstasy, heroin…

Lautaro had started with his father's business—cocaine manufacturing plants outside Aldao, San Pedro, and Gastre, with distribution channels throughout South America and into North America. He'd expanded the business to incorporate other drugs like heroin from Asia and ecstasy from the Netherlands. Then, Luminous from Chicago.

Controlling distribution channels had opened the door for him to work with Poindexter Pharmaceutical. Lautaro owned and operated the expansive network to distribute the company's failed trial narcotic—though he had to commend whoever was behind the arrangement at the drug company on their ingenuity. Poindexter Pharmaceutical was recuperating millions of research and development dollars by selling the drug on the streets. Well, the company and most of the investors weren't reaping that ROI. Probably only a few select conspirators were lining their pockets, but such was business. Lautaro didn't know the names of those involved, since all of his interactions were through the Shoup Group.

He was aware that they were working to build an undisclosed facility to move drug production before the FDA inevitably shut down the drug trial. Lautaro's role was to silence those who would blow the whistle before the transfer happened.

At last, he was inside the warmth of his limo. He would rest at the Ritz-Carlton tonight and rent a car tomorrow.

He called Dom. "I'm in Chicago."

"How will you find the doctor? I've not had any success locating her through our usual contacts."

His brother referred to the infrastructure to find people through electronic means. But Dr. Ong would be smart enough to move around by electronically undetectable means. And if she wasn't, her private security, former-Ranger bodyguard would be.

"Simple," Lautaro said. "The only reason for her to go to Chicago is to investigate the source of the drug. I simply wait for her to arrive at Poindexter Pharmaceutical."

"She has family in Chicago. You could use them as leverage."

"I'll make that my secondary plan if things fail at the research center."

"Are you coordinating with Shoup?"

"No," he snapped. "I will close the loop on this problem myself."

WHILE REECE WENT shopping for supplies, Jess called Jenna.

"Jess! We got your shifts covered now through the twenty-eighth. It's in an email. And I have some interesting news."

"Any distraction is good," Jess said flatly.

"I dug a little deeper on Mrs. Monroe—the acute lung injury

patient. Turns out soccer mom was taking more than prescription oxycodone for her shoulder pain. I had her husband dig around the house, and he found some pills in a bag. I'm betting it's your trial drug—well, the illegal version."

Jess frowned into the phone. "I guess Luminous has infiltrated suburbia."

Silence stretched between them for a beat.

"Shit's getting real," Jess said on an exhale.

"Please stay safe," Jenna said.

"You remember that time you were going into danger and told me to look after Cal if anything happened to you?"

"Stop, Jess."

"Yeah, I'm not laying some ridiculous obligation on you like that because I'm a better friend." She also had no children.

Jenna chuckled, and Jess took a moment to enjoy the sound.

Jess continued, "I don't even have a pet for you to look after if something happens to me. I should make you buy one in my honor."

"You're going to be fine," Jenna said so firmly she almost convinced Jess for a moment.

"I do have this peace lily though. It's gorgeous, and since it's the only plant I haven't managed to kill, it'd be great if you could take care of it."

Jenna let out a huff. "I would smack you right now if I was in Chicago with you. I know you're making jokes, but you're actually scared. I'm telling you—the Rider team has your back."

"I trust Reece. I feel like we're closer because of this, but it isn't real."

"You're referring to your feelings for each other?"

"Oh, mine are real. I'm only referring to his. Maybe they're real, but if he can't commit to a long-term relationship..." Her voice trailed off.

"If he doesn't grab on to you with both hands and commit to a long-term relationship when this is over, then you know it isn't real. He doesn't know what he's missing."

Jess swallowed and wiped her eyes. "Did I ever tell you he's never said 'I love you'?"

"Yeah, you did. You want me to tell my husband to beat up his best friend?" Jenna's voice dropped to a conspiratorial whisper.

Jess sniffed. "Okay. Game face. I need to focus. Can't worry about a nonexistent relationship if I'm not alive."

"Jessica Ong!" Jenna snapped.

"Just remember to water my damn plant. I love you." She clicked the phone off.

REECE RETURNED to the rental home with supplies. He set the plastic bags on the kitchen table and placed a bouquet of roses beside them.

Jess sifted through the clothing. "Black spandex! We're going to look like burglars, not researchers."

He shook out a white lab coat and gave her a look of satisfaction.

Her lips quirked. "You know, most researchers leave their lab coats at the office. We'll look unusual walking from the parking lot into the building wearing them."

He took her chin in his hand and planted a kiss on her lips. "Then let's hope low-tier, weekend night-shift security guards don't consider that level of minutia. Let's hope they see professionals who entered via the employee route with a badge and think nothing more of it."

She conceded his point with a nod before turning her attention to the flowers. "Are you wooing me, or are these for my funeral? Because I'm partial to sunflowers."

He scowled as he laid the lab coat over one chair. "Neither. They will be delivered during our entry as a distraction."

"A dozen red roses? I'm sure the florist could have arranged the delivery themselves. You didn't have to bring them here first."

"Are you going to get dressed or pick apart every aspect of my plan?"

She ran her fingers over the red petals. "I'm sorry. You're right. I trust you. I'm just nervous." She gathered up her clothes, turned, and left.

Reece watched her go. She had a right to be nervous. They were venturing into danger where a company stood to lose millions of dollars and face criminal charges if Jess succeeded in proving her theory—Lori Sullivan's theory. Whoever was behind the theft at Poindexter Pharmaceutical would want to silence both of them—permanently.

He pulled a small brick of C-4 out of his weapons bag. The organic explosive, RDX, was combined with a plastic binder and plasticizer for malleability. The ingredients were mixed in dissolved form and the solvent extracted in a drying and filtering process. The final solid C-4 product was putty-like and smelled like motor oil. Reece liked to use the explosive for how stable it was; it wouldn't be detonated by dropping it, shooting it, setting it on fire, or sticking it in a microwave. Only the little detonator he inserted would initiate the necessary shock wave when he activated it remotely.

He rigged it to a trigger device and worked quickly to conceal it before Jess reemerged from changing clothes. She didn't need to know about the explosive. He hoped he'd never have to use it.

He holstered his gun as she reappeared dressed in all black.

"One more thing." He withdrew a bullet-resistant vest and held it up for her.

"It's huge."

"I believe you've mentioned that before." He winked at her.

She pursed her lips and placed a hand on her hip even as her cheeks pinked. "I was referring to the vest."

"Ah, right." He slipped it on her and began tightening the straps.

"More like a dress than a vest," she complained.

He smiled. "Then that's more of you covered." He stood back, surveying his work. He pulled on the white lab coat to top off the look.

She moved stiffly. "I feel like an overstuffed dumpling in a stale wrapper."

He bunched the coat collar in his hands and pulled her toward him as he bent lower. Nose to nose, he said, "You're beautiful. And now you're protected. If I'm going to take you into danger tonight, I need to know you're protected. The vest doesn't come off until I say it does."

"Okay. Okay." She rolled her shoulders as he released her. "No taking off the straightjacket—I mean, bullet-proof vest."

"Bullet-resistant. Not bulletproof."

She tugged at the vest. "You never told me you were into S and M."

He leveled his gaze at her. "I'm into keeping you alive."

21

---

*A*s they drove to Poindexter Pharmaceutical, Jess reflected on the last few days. Prior to this fiasco, the most danger she'd faced was from a needlestick or infectious disease. She'd never felt hunted like an animal—until now.

She'd never shot anyone, and still wondered if she'd lose her medical license if her act was discovered. Surely the evil villain wouldn't report the assault to authorities when he was guilty of his own acts of violence.

Now, she was going to break into private property. If they were caught without the proof they needed against the pharma company, they could go to jail. Even she couldn't make light of that possibility by joking about how terrible she looked in orange. Would she be an easy target in prison? A shank to the chest and no more Jessica Ong.

The car began to feel hot and cramped as Reece pulled into the parking lot. She shoved the vent slats on the dash to blow the heat away from her.

Think of something else, anything else, she willed herself. She thought of Reece tonight, fixing her tea one last time before they left. He was showing his love. He'd been showering her with it for the last three days. As much as she wanted to believe his actions were a sign of changing times, she couldn't let herself become vulnerable again.

I can't do this without you.

His words rang in her ears like a soothing tune, giving her strength and resolve.

She fiddled with the collar of the lab coat—the bullet-resistant vest a continuous reminder of the danger they could encounter. Reece wore his bullet-resistant pants and blazer with his cowboy boots. He even had a pair of fake glasses to make him appear scholarly. He looked far more stylish than she did.

Hmm. That was a first.

She was armed with only her phone and an encrypted USB—the same one that Lori Sullivan had sent her. She wasn't sure if she would need it in order to download any information she found at the research facility. But the computers in there were probably password-protected. However, Reece had given her a second USB—one programmed to plant spyware on the system which would enable Claire to access the hard drive.

Reece parked in the employee lot and turned off the engine. Only a few other cars were present on a Saturday evening. Jess stared out at the layer of white powder covering the lawn. In the parking lot, the snow had been plowed to the far outside corners. Above them, the deepest blue night sky twinkled with stars.

"You need to review the plan?" Reece asked.

"No. I'm good."

She felt the heat from his intense gaze as he sized her up. He was probably trying to gauge if she was going to keep her shit together when danger reared its ugly head.

She stared back at him, unblinking. "I'm good," she repeated firmly.

"I love you." He leaned in for a kiss on her lips before turning and getting out of the car.

Jess's cheeks flushed, and she sputtered, "What?" The ability to form a coherent sentence abandoned her.

She exited the car and scrambled to follow Reece toward the building. Her temper rose. He couldn't just say something like that in the middle of this type of crisis when they had no time to discuss it.

Her rational brain wanted to tear into him about the inappropriateness of his timing, and her irrational heart soared like an eagle on the wind. His declaration sounded like a huge step, but she needed to not get ahead of herself. *I love you* in the middle of a stressful situation didn't translate into *I will spend Christmas with your family.* And those three little words couldn't guarantee they would even survive the night.

She clamped her mouth shut and gave Reece one more glare as she swiped Zabner's key card. With a twinkle in his eye and a twitch of his mustache, Reece opened the EMPLOYEES ONLY door. They walked toward the stairs, nothing stealthy but trying not to draw attention to themselves either.

At the front desk, the security guard verbally pushed back against the delivery of a dozen red roses.

"There's no one here by that name," the guard said.

"Well, dude, this is the address I have. I get paid to deliver to the address. If the address is wrong, it's not my fault."

"Well, among other things, I get paid to take deliveries, but I'm not allowed to except deliveries for employees who don't work here."

"I delivered, man. Throw them in the trash or take them home to your wife."

Jess and Reece stepped into the stairwell as the deliveryman was leaving the building. They climbed the steps silently to the second floor and moved from room to room. As Jess looked for stores of medication or portals of computers to access, Reece remained on alert for any danger.

The hallways were long and sterile. Harsh fluorescent lights stretched in long beams above them. Light grayish-green walls contrasted the dark-gray mosaic pattern of the laminated flooring.

In one office, Jess located a computer with Ethernet access. She tapped a few keys to pull it out of sleep mode and inserted the USB. "How do we know if it's working?"

"It's working," he assured her. "Let's keep moving."

"We're just going to leave it there, sticking out like a sore thumb?"

"Once it works its magic, it will erase itself. It won't be traced back to Rider SI."

They continued to search for what seemed like an interminably long amount of time.

Reece looked at his watch. "I'm so glad we brought the researcher along so she could point us directly to the evil scientist's lab."

"Hey, I'm doing my best here." She glowered at him.

"Given a little more advanced notice, Claire would have had this place mapped out down to the ventilation system."

They came to a door that required badge and key card access.

"This looks promising," she said. She swiped Zabner's card and tried the door. "Nope. Need a code in addition to the key card. Every code in my hospital is a four-digit number."

"Jess—"

"And they usually keep it simple." She tried one-two-three-four-star. Nothing happened. "Let's see what numbers are worn." She fished her phone out and turned on the flashlight.

"Jess—"

"The two looks worn." She tried two-two-two-two-star, but nothing happened.

"Jess—"

"What?" she snapped. "You have a better idea?"

He picked her up by the hips and moved her aside. "It's called the boot bypass."

"Boot bypass? Like a reboot? You have a device for that?"

"Not exactly." He plucked the keycard from her hand and swiped it again. As the light turned from green to red, he took a step back. He drew his leg up to his chest then rocketed it forward and struck the door with his boot where the lock anchored it. The wood splintered around the frame. When he struck a second time, it opened with the cracking of wood and snapping of metal.

"Boot bypass." He gestured toward the entrance.

Jess cringed. "What if you'd set off an alarm?"

He passed the keycard back to her. "The key *card* de-activated the alarm. The key*pad* is only for the lock."

They entered a room lined with shelves containing boxes. She turned her phone flashlight on and shone it over the labels.

"Let's try this one." Reece reached over her, pulled the box down, and set it on an empty countertop. He produced a knife from his pocket and cut open the tape sealing the cardboard. After reaching inside, he withdrew an aluminum rectangle.

"Is this it?" He handed it to her.

She inspected the blister pack. "Trihydrodone. Yes." The packs had the name, manufacturer, and warning label that the contents were a study drug and not yet FDA approved for use. She took pictures of the box and blister pack.

"I expected something grander," Reece said.

"Like maybe they'd glow in the dark or be covered in biohazard signs? Or skull and crossbones?"

"Where are the orange pill bottles?"

"Those come from the pharmacies after they count them out of larger jars. These are probably in this arrangement for easy distribution in the trial. No miscounts can happen during distribution to patients, and study coordinators can easily see how many pills have been taken and how many are left."

Reece froze, listening.

Jess heard the clicking of heels down the hallway approaching them.

AFTER LAUTARO RECEIVED a phone call informing him that people matching the pictures of Reece Owen and Dr. Ong had arrived at the Poindexter complex, he drove a rented BMW to the scene.

He dismissed the informant—unsure if the man was trustworthy enough to keep his mouth shut if he witnessed Lautaro killing the doctor and the cowboy. The watchman had served his purpose of idly monitoring the place so Lautaro wouldn't have to sit in a car for half a day while his mind and butt went numb. He needed to be sharp for the showdown. And he'd needed a weapon. He'd spent two hours tracking down a place to buy the gun and bullets he needed.

As he lay in wait, he kept the car idling for warmth and a quick getaway. He loaded his Ruger P89 with hollow-point bullets and oxidized copper jacket. When they struck their target, the slugs created sharp talons to cut through organs. And the bullets could pierce Kevlar. A private security group like Rider SI would ensure they wore protection. Lautaro would ensure he bypassed it. For Dom.

Brass bullets could also pierce body armor and had to be Teflon-coated to protect the gun from the hardened brass casing.

Lautaro preferred the oxidized copper jackets mostly because black was a cool color for bullets.

Successfully stopping Dr. Ong served many purposes. Lautaro needed to save face within his organization and the Shoup Group, owing to his men's failure to seize her in Atlanta. Thwarting her would ensure the supply of lucrative, highly addictive narcotic would keep flowing. And lastly, he would show current and future business partners his resolve when facing a challenge.

In the opposite parking lot, several obsidian Ford Explorers pulled in and came to a screeching halt. A dozen men dressed in black poured out of the vehicles and into the Poindexter building. Shoup's men, no doubt.

Mierda!

Yes, and there was the man himself, bringing up the rear. Large and bald and clearly giving the orders. Didn't his head get cold in the Chicago winter air? Lautaro shivered.

Shoup lifted his nose into the cold night air, like a wolf sniffing for danger. Then he turned and faced Lautaro's vehicle, eyes squinting in a massive round face.

Lautaro swore.

Shoup walked toward him as he took out a cigar and lit it. The smoke was quickly whisked away by the breeze. When the man was a few feet away, Lautaro rolled down his window. As Shoup leaned forward and exhaled, the stench of cigar smoke filled Lautaro's BMW.

He wrinkled his nose. "A little early for a victory cigar."

"What are you doing here, Fernandez?" His voice was thick and gravelly, as if his vocal cords had been seared by the foul thing hanging between his lips. His square jaw held a five-o'clock shadow.

"Watching the show. Front-row seats."

Shoup glanced down at the gun in the passenger seat. "So long as you don't plan on coming onstage."

Lautaro's gaze slid to the building where Shoup's men were spreading out on the ground floor. "The man in that building shot my brother."

Shoup snorted. "A flesh wound. Surely you're not going to let that cloud your judgment and interfere with your business partnership."

Lautaro grit his teeth. Maybe this *cerdo* had no sense of honor and loyalty to family, but Lautaro did. He resisted the urge to look at his gun and betray his thoughts. How easy would it be to reach for the weapon, point, and shoot?

Then Shoup wouldn't be so flippant and dismissive. Lautaro could teach him a lesson. But he couldn't let his temper dictate his next move. He was up against a Ranger who'd bested Lautaro's men several times. Shoup and his men stood a better chance of defeating Reece Owen.

"Stay in the car, Fernandez." With that, Shoup turned and walked toward the building.

It seemed Lautaro might not be given his opportunity at redemption. Still, Shoup might underestimate the Rider security expert as Lautaro's men had done... as Dom had done.

Lautaro would lie in wait, he decided, and see what opportunity arose. If he positioned himself near Dr. Ong's getaway vehicle —*a Honda Accord of all things!*—he could be prepared to pounce should the targets escape Shoup.

***

"EXCUSE ME, what do you think you're doing here?" A woman's surprised and harsh voice cut through the silence of the hallway.

Before Jess had time to even process her surprise or generate a coherent and logical excuse for their intrusion in the building, Reece sprang into action.

The woman's eyes registered fear as he stepped toward her and smoothly positioned himself beside her. He fluidly spun her around and brought her back against his chest while clamping one hand over her mouth even as she opened it to scream. He wrapped his other hand around her neck.

Silently, she flailed for a moment, still trying to scream as she clawed at his arms. But she wouldn't make a dent or scratch in his special suit. Her face reddened as her frightened wide eyes began to close.

Finally, she went lax, but Jess was still shaking at the violent scene. She knew the terror the woman must have experienced with a man's large arm around her neck.

Reece dragged the woman's lax body to one of the storage rooms. He pulled out a plastic twist tie and secured her hands and legs.

When he rejoined Jess in the hallway, he narrowed his eyes at her as if she'd accused him of something. "She'll be all right."

Jess understood he'd asphyxiated her to the point of unconsciousness, not death, but it still scared her. "'All right' is relative. She's going to have nightmares about you."

"Better she loses a little sleep over a few bad dreams then we face certain death if she sounds the alarm."

"You don't know that she is a part of this."

"You don't know that she isn't," he fired back. "Even if she isn't, we're trespassing in her workplace. I'm sure she's been trained to notify security of unauthorized intruders." Reece shook his head. "I'll be sure to send my condolences in a Christmas card."

They made their way back toward the stairwell in hopes of a speedy exit.

22

Reece checked his watch—sixty-two minutes had elapsed since their entry. It certainly wasn't his fastest burglary, but they'd accomplished their goal.

As they walked back toward the stairwell, he lamented not having a full team for this mission. With time and planning, he would have had two more Rider teammates in the building with them and another in the getaway vehicle. Claire would be parked a few blocks away, and everyone would be linked through com devices. Good missions ran like rehearsed orchestras—like the time they took down Lucius Titan. Harmony, precision, perfection. Mission accomplished.

At the door to the stairs, Reece moved in front of Jess. "Normally, I'd say ladies first, but we don't know what awaits us on the other side of that door."

"After you."

Before he pushed it open, the elevator midway down the hall dinged. Reece pressed their bodies against the wall and peered back down the corridor. In the distance, men in black fatigues stormed onto the floor and fanned out.

Gun in one his hand at his side, Reece pushed open the door with the other. The stairwell was silent—not yet breeched. Jess followed him, and they descended the stairs. Reece listened for the sound of doors opening above or below them.

When they reached the ground floor, he cracked the door open to peer at their predicament in the lobby. Shouts erupted as five men in black fatigues rushed him.

"Run!" he yelled at Jess.

The exit was just ten feet from them, and nothing stood in Jess's path in that direction. She had the car keys in her lab coat. She could make it to the Honda and drive away.

He'd buy her time.

His vision narrowed as blood pumped adrenaline through his body. He spun and ducked, firing his weapon into arms and legs. Every one of his shots took down an attacker. Their bullets either missed or didn't penetrate his suit. Since most were glancing blows, the pain didn't slow him down.

He suspected the men had a "do not kill" order since no one was aiming for his head. They probably wanted to know how far the breach of Poindexter Pharmaceutical's indiscretions had spread before they killed Jess and him.

From behind him, the men from the second floor exited the stairwell and joined the fight, but Reece was out of bullets. One of the men jumped on his back. Reece bent his legs and flung him over his shoulder. Another struck Reece in the back of the head with the butt of a gun while Reece was still bent low.

He faltered, giving his attackers a precious second to gain the advantage. Three men restrained him.

"Stop!"

Fury and despair filled Reece at the sound of Jess's voice. She was supposed to be gone and out of harm's way by now.

"Damn stubborn woman," he growled, pinned on his knees with two men wrenching his arms behind his back and the cold metal muzzle of a gun pressed to his head. He stilled, taking in the dismal scene as he panted from the exertion.

The Shoup Group had brought a dozen men. Five were writhing on the ground, injured from Reece's attack. Two had his arms, one held the gun on him. Four more stood behind him.

A large bald man with enormous biceps stepped out from behind the men and stared at Jess who stood by the door, phone in hand.

Mr. Shoup, Reece knew from the profile Claire had assembled, looked back and forth from Reece to Jess. The smirk on his pair of overly plump lips indicated that he now understood their intimate relationship.

"Nobody move, or I'm going to press send on my phone." For a small woman, her voice carried loudly through the entry room. Reece imagined this was the commanding tone she used to run a cardiac arrest in the hospital. "If I press send, all of the information about Luminous and trihydrodone gets sent to my brother."

Recognition flashed in Shoup's eyes. He would have done his due diligence in background checks and known Jess's brother was an investigative reporter.

Reece wanted to scream at her in frustration. Her gamble could backfire. Shoup could just decide to kill the two of them and then send a team after her brother to silence him before he could do any damage.

"That's right," Jess continued. "Poindexter Pharmaceutical will go under when proof linking the trial drug to the street drug—and the deadly side effects of both—is revealed."

Shoup crossed his arms over a large barrel chest and stared at Jess.

"Give me Reece, and I'll give you my phone," she said.

He lowered his head in defeat. This was a terrible idea. Didn't she understand that Shoup would kill them both anyway?

When he raised his head again, a single tear streamed down Jess's cheek even as her eyes burned with determination.

Yes, she understands, Reece realized.

She knew staying was a death sentence, which meant she'd already sent the information to her brother—which wasn't complete without the mass spectrometry comparison of each drug but might be enough to prompt authorities to launch a full investigation.

So why had she stayed if she knew she wouldn't survive? He thought about one of the mornings they'd spent on her couch after a long shift. He'd massaged her feet while she drank decaf green tea. She'd told him she'd lost two patients that night, and she thought perhaps one of the saddest things she witnessed in her career was someone dying alone. If her dying patient didn't have family present, Jess would stay to make sure they didn't slip off into the light of the unknown without anyone to comfort them.

Tonight, she'd stayed because she didn't want Reece to die alone, even if it meant... His throat threatened to close shut with dread and agony.

Shoup pulled his weapon out of his holster and fired.

"No!" Reece screamed.

Jess's small body flew backward and landed on the floor near the employee exit door.

Another shot rang out, this one coming from outside the building and shattering a front pane window. The man holding a gun to Reece's head collapsed. The second one restraining Reece went down with the next shot fired.

Shoup crouched, holstered his weapon, and dashed toward Jess, who lay on the floor. He scooped up her phone beside her limp body and exited through the employee door.

Reece spun out of the grip of the man holding him and landed a solid punch to his jaw. He snatched his gun up and holstered it as he sprinted to Jess. He needed to get them out of the building because when Shoup's men regained their wits, they would open fire.

Reaching Jess, he lifted her into his arms. As soon as he was out the door, he pressed the detonation button in his pocket for the C-4 he'd planted in the base of the bouquet of roses sitting on the front desk.

A deafening explosion erupted as glass rained down on them.

MICA CALLED DORIAN. She didn't want to interrupt a mission, but the suspense was killing her. Last she'd heard, Ryan and Santino had arrived in Chicago and were picking up supplies before heading to Poindexter's research facility. Dorian had already arrived and had set up, perched in a tree.

"Mica," Dorian greeted her over the phone.

"Any updates?" She paced her living room.

"Yes, I'm entirely too old to play the role of sniper cover." His voice was a smooth British accent with the steady hum of wind in the background.

"I'd put you on a different assignment, but I don't know your full background yet." Mica didn't know what career Dorian had had before joining the Rider team, only that she suspected it had been something highly covert involving now redacted files.

His silence as a reply told her she wouldn't get that information out of him anytime soon.

"Any updates on the mission?"

"Ah, yes, that. Well, Dr. Ong and Reece were in the building long enough, I hope they obtained the sample they sought. Mr. Shoup's team arrived as I was rushing to set up my weapon."

A lump formed in her throat. "Is anyone hurt?"

"Reece took a beating, and Dr. Ong was shot."

Mica sank into her recliner, nausea sweeping through her.

"Mr. Shoup shot her. I couldn't get a clear line of sight on him, but I took out a few others, and Reece was able to get Dr. Ong out of the building before he detonated an explosive."

"*Dang.* Are they alive?"

"I'm looking through my scope lens now. They're lying on the asphalt but talking to each other. So, yes, both alive. I believe she was shot in the vest."

"Thank heavens."

"There isn't much left of the Shoup crew, but Mr. Shoup is escaping. You want me to finish him?"

"No. We need to get our own out of there and cover our tracks."

She heard the sound of clicks and sliding metal as if Dorian was dismantling his rifle.

"Done. I'll see you at the debriefing."

"Thank you, Dorian."

Alive. Everyone on their team was alive.

Mica breathed a sigh of relief. Miracles did happen.

* * *

REECE CROUCHED, keeping his body protectively over Jess's until the wave of heat and flying debris subsided. The entire world seemed to shake, although he knew he'd only used a small amount that would mostly just annihilate the front desk.

His ears were ringing, and the taste of metal filled his mouth as he drew back from Jess.

Her eyes fluttered open. "You brought fireworks for me?" Her strained voice indicated she was still in pain from the gunshot to her vest, even though she hadn't lost her sense of humor.

"Damn stubborn woman." He scowled at her even as he lowered his mouth to hers. He kissed her lips, her neck, and her ear even as he scolded her. "Next time I tell you to run, you run." Seeing her shot—even knowing it was center chest into the vest—had almost killed him. "I'll chain you in the basement if I have to in order to keep you safe." He nuzzled his face into her neck.

"You don't have a basement."

"I'll build one."

"What are you going to do with me while I'm chained up?" Her voice was a teasing invitation, but it didn't completely mask the quiver of fear beneath.

He let out a low growl as he breathed warm air onto the exposed skin at the base of her neck.

She chuckled. "As much as I like the attention, I'd like to get off the hard asphalt and out of the cold."

After a final quick, firm kiss on her lips, he helped her stand.

A van pulled into the lot, and Ryan slid open the door, motioning to them. Reece and Jess walked toward the van, both moving slowly from the pain of having been shot. Reece's back protested, and the rest of his body would be even more black-and-blue tomorrow from the fight.

A man sprung up from behind the Honda rental and took aim. He had menacing dark eyes and a face contorted with some mixture of rage and diabolical glee. With an arm around Jess, Reece was in no position to shoot first.

Ryan fired, and the gunman spun to the ground—a bullet in

his shoulder. He hopped out of the van and kicked Lautaro's gun away from him.

"Your timing is fortuitous, Walsh," Reece said, helping Jess up into the van.

"Oh, I don't know. Seems like we needed to get here sooner," Ryan said. "I'm sorry you were shot, Jess." He stood over Lautaro, keeping his gun trained on him.

Reece climbed in the van. "We're alive because of you." He noted Santino in the driver's seat and gave him a grateful nod. "Who was the sniper?"

"Dorian."

"He was phenomenal." He leaned back in the seat, exhausted and grateful to be alive. He had a great deal to be thankful for this Christmas.

"Keys," Ryan said.

Reece tossed the rental car keys to him. His partner climbed in the Honda rental and drove away.

Reece helped Jess struggle out of her vest. This had been one of the bloodiest, most violent encounters he'd had since joining Rider Sl. He'd have a lot of explaining to do and would likely be jailed for manslaughter if any of Shoup's men died in the explosion. But that would be an inquisition and a court battle for another day.

Today, he needed rest and sleep. He leaned back and closed his eyes, pulling Jess against him as Santino drove them out of the parking lot.

23

———

Reece and Jess arrived back at the rental with shopping bags in hand. Once inside, he set the results of Jess's spending spree on the table. She'd said Christmas would be just immediate family, but she'd bought enough gifts for a small platoon. He'd been content to carry her bags and watch her expression light up as she bought presents for her parents, brother, and nieces.

They'd spent the first two days after the harrowing events at the research lab recovering from the physical trauma. During that time, he'd completed his full report to Mica. Now, it was a waiting game to see if the FBI came knocking with evidence of his and Jess's involvement.

When his hands were free, Jess stepped into his arms. "Thank you for agreeing to go to my family Christmas."

"It's long overdue. Thank you for taking me back." He'd been a fool to let her go before and would never let it happen again. He didn't understand why she loved him, but he was prepared to spend the rest of his life enjoying her affections while trying to figure it out.

She bit her lip. "My mom can be a little overbearing."

He unzipped her coat and peeled it off to reveal her pink sweater beneath. He tossed her coat aside and removed his.

"I'm sure I'll manage." He smiled.

"And Jay's kids can be a little wild."

He hoisted her up so she sat on the counter, and he situated himself between her thighs. He hadn't seduced her in a few days because they were both recovering—him from the fighting and her from the bullet contusion.

"I'm unconcerned about boisterous children." He lifted her sweater over her head and pressed his lips to the soft skin above her clavicle.

She sucked in a breath.

"Move in with me," he said—not a question and a little too demanding to be a plea. He kissed his way to her shoulder as he moved her bra strap out of the path of his lips. "Move in with me and stay in Atlanta. We'll come visit your family as often as you like."

She fisted her hand in his hair as she wrapped her legs around his waist.

"Move in with me," he repeated, bending lower and kissing the tender bruise between her breasts. "Half the rooms I finished with you in mind."

"And the hot tub?" She bunched his shirt and pulled it off over his head.

"That's for both of us to enjoy together."

She raked her fingers down his chest. "I'll move in with you."

He drew back and cupped her face with his hands, making unwavering eye contact. Her cheeks were flushed and her mouth was slightly parted.

"I love you, Jess."

As he kissed her, her body melted against him, and she purred softly. She wrapped her arms around him, and he lifted her into the air, carrying her to the bedroom.

MICA SAT in the coffee shop across from FBI Special Agent Eddie Finch. He wore a pressed navy suit, and his dark hair was coiffed. His sunglasses were off and laying on the table between them.

"Another impressive case," Eddie said.

Mica fluffed the pink scarf around her neck. "Thanks." She'd handed him three career-making cases: AJ Shlau who worked for Lucius Titan, then Lucius himself, and now Poindexter Pharmaceutical—or whichever employees they discovered behind the conspiracy.

"Lying creates loose ends though," Eddie added, a slightly accusatory edge to his tone.

Mica gave him a knowing grin. A by-the-book agent like Eddie didn't like lying and certainly abhorred loose ends.

"My people are good people. I'll continue to protect them."

"I can tell. No weapons belonging to anyone on the Rider team were found on the scene at the research center, so your people can't be placed there."

Mica said nothing. Her team knew how to be careful. Eddie would speculate but never know the extent of the Rider team's involvement.

"All of the security footage from Poindexter Pharmaceutical was erased by someone," Eddie added.

"Maybe it was destroyed in the explosion," she said, knowing Claire had covered their tracks by erasing the footage.

"Dr. Jessica Ong," Eddie continued, "maintains that she and

Reece Owen came to Chicago to spend Christmas with her family. Her brother, who wrote a rather detailed and accurate article linking the trial drug to the illegal narcotic, is hiding behind his right to protect his confidential source."

Mica sipped her caramel latte and shrugged. "We did our job and delivered the incriminating information." Since the truth had come to light through Jay's article, the Shoup Group had abandoned their pursuit of Dr. Ong.

The slight narrowing of Eddie's eyes betrayed his disbelief in Mica's assertions. "There was a lot of unexplained blood in the entryway at Poindexter Pharmaceutical."

That's a relief, Mica thought. Men had likely died there, according to Reece, but if only blood was found, then the Shoup Group probably removed the bodies of their own so they wouldn't be implicated.

Eddie's voice grew harder as he added, "And I have rumors of the Fernandez brothers involvement in drug distribution, but they've fled back to South America."

"What do you want me to do? Sing the *You're Welcome* song?"

He gave her a puzzled look. Of course, the man had probably never watched a Disney movie in his life. Mica, on the other hand, was obligated to watch them all, since she now had a child—even if her son wasn't old enough to watch them yet.

Eddie poked a finger in Mica's direction. "Jessica Ong is involved in this somehow."

"I don't know what to tell you, Eddie. Our records are called the *Sullivan File* for a reason—not the Ong File. We followed Dr. Sullivan's dying request to help bring her research to light. We gave her USB to Jay Ong along with the mass spectrometry results proving Luminous and trihydrodone are one and the same drug. Dr. Sullivan's work and Jay Ong's investigation revealed the conspiracy, which as you said is now a detailed publication. You have your bad guy wrapped up with a bow on top."

Almost. It was up to the FBI to find the exact perpetrator or perpetrators within Poindexter Pharmaceutical.

Eddie leaned back and crossed his arms, appearing lost in contemplation. "I do. And I'm grateful. You could have not informed the FBI about Jay Ong's plans for releasing his article or you could have told the Chicago office and not me."

Mica stifled her surprise. Eddie usually took the gift-wrapped villains she gave him as something she was obligated to do as a responsible citizen, rather than something she had an option to do.

"Still, this was sloppy work, Mica. I've got two dead Poindexter employees—one in Atlanta by car bomb, one in Chicago by gunshot. I'm pretty sure people died at Poindexter Pharmaceutical based on the crime scene blood—maybe their bodies will wash up in Lake Michigan in a week. And you're sitting there smug like Rider SI isn't neck-deep in this mess."

Mica crossed her arms. Eddie hadn't also listed Lautaro's injuries. He and his brother would be seeking revenge on the Rider team, and thought weighed heavily on her.

"You've heard of the Shoup Group?" Mica asked.

Eddie picked up his sunglasses, pulled out a handkerchief from his blazer, and began to clean the lenses. "Sure, private security like you."

"Not like my company. More like Titan Enterprises was but more black ops and less direct involvement in crimes."

"Criminal protection?"

"For wealthy criminals, yes."

"You're saying they're involved in this?"

"You won't find any proof—other than unexplained funds drifting out of the account of whoever is behind the Luminous conspiracy at Poindexter. But, yes, the Shoup Group is involved. So, I've got bigger problems than you telling me someone fighting for his life was maybe a little 'sloppy.'" She folded her hands on the table and leaned forward. "You go up against a dozen armed ex-military men and let's see if things don't get a little 'sloppy.'"

Eddie stood and slipped on his glasses. "I follow the rules, which means I won't ever be in a ridiculous situation like that."

"Which means you won't ever win against the bad guys without us helping you out."

His hardened jaw told her she'd struck a nerve. She watched him leave, knowing he was digesting her bitter truth. Without getting his hands dirty, Eddie would never close a case the way Rider SI did. But she needed him—needed him to follow through on ensuring the criminals she compiled evidence against were taken to prosecution. Maybe she shouldn't have pointed out his weakness so bluntly, but she wouldn't silently tolerate him criticizing her team.

Her phone dinged. She pulled it out of her jeans and read the text from weapons developer and longtime Rider SI client Bill Sharp.

Ava is missing. Can you help?

Mica's stomach plummeted. Ava his daughter. While Mica's team protected Bill Sharp directly, they only kept tabs on his daughter from a distance, since she had declined bodyguards. Ava was traveling to South America to pick up a new breeding stallion, and Mica had her itinerary saved in an email from Bill.

Mica, *Where was she last seen?*

Bill, *Last texted me from Buenos Aires.*

Mica, *I'm on it.*

Her mind already racing, she knew the Alonso brothers were right for the task. Rafe was already in South America, and she could send Santino to assist. Bill Sharp had many dubious enemies, but the Alonso brothers were raised mostly in South America. If Ava was still alive, they'd find her.

———

JESS WALKED beside Reece up the steps to her parents' house. He carried a stack of festively wrapped presents.

Glowing golden lights framed the edges of the house and the bushes in the yard, while twinkling red-and-white candy canes decorated the pathway from the sidewalk to the front door.

"Are you humming *My Favorite Things*?" he asked.

"Maybe," she said sweetly.

"Because that's not a Christmas song."

"Of course, it is. I have a Christmas ornament that plays the tune." Jess rang the doorbell and waited, bopping up and down on her tiptoes—partially from excitement and partially from the cold.

"Clearly your trinket was commercialized." Reece stood beside her looking dapper in jeans, boots, and his leather jacket. Exhaled wisps of cold air curled around his mustache before drifting higher and being swept away by the chilly air.

"'Warm woolen mittens,' 'silver white winters', 'brown paper packages tied up with string.' Sounds like Christmas," she countered.

"Julie Andrews is listing her favorite things. Doesn't make it a Christmas song. It isn't sung in musical during Christmas."

Jess detected the teasing tone in his voice, but this was a disagreement she intended to win. "Fine. Then *Die Hard* isn't a Christmas movie."

He insisted they watch the Bruce Willis movie every holiday in exchange for him watching *Miracle on 34ᵗʰ Street* with her.

"Darling," he drawled, "that's just blasphemy."

"Just because the action film takes place at a Christmas party doesn't make it a Christmas movie."

Reece smiled. "I suppose we've reached an accord. I will grant *My Favorite Things* as a Christmas song if you grant *Die Hard* as a Christmas movie."

"Agreed." She winked, feeling his smile radiate sunshine through her.

"Jessica!" Her mom swung the door wide and pulled her into a hug. "Oh my. You wore your high heels." She looked up at Jess and wrinkled her nose.

Jess chuckled. "They are platforms, Mom, and my boyfriend is six two. I have to add height."

"And here he is!" She looked around the presents. "I guess you aren't a myth."

"No, ma'am."

"Come in, come in. Don't want you to die of cold exposure when we finally meet you."

Warmth and the smell of pecan pie engulfed Jess as they entered, and her mom closed the door. Reece walked to the Christmas tree and placed the presents with the others before returning to Jess's side. He rested an arm over her shoulder as if sensing her need for reassurance. With him by her side, her world shone brighter than Chicago's Millennium Park Christmas tree. He was finally at her home and meeting her family—and on Christmas no less. The occasion felt perfect.

"Jess!" Jay walked into the room, and she left Reece's side to skip into her brother's arms.

"Merry Christmas."

Jay squeezed her tight, pulled back from the embrace, and grinned. "Christmas came early with the dynamite story you gave me."

"Story? I didn't give you a story." She batted her eyelashes.

"Lori Sullivan did." She backed up until she was beside Reece again.

"Right. And I'm Santa Claus."

His two girls sprinted into the room and wrapped Jess in hugs, almost knocking her down. "Aunt Jess!"

She laughed and lowered her voice to Jay. "I mean, you kind of are." She winked at him.

Ouch. The impact of the girls' collision had struck Jess in the sternum—right where her enormous bruise was from the gunshot wound.

"I bet *your* story would have been even more amazing," Jay said.

"Anna and Vivienne, this is my friend Reece Owen," she said, changing the subject.

They giggled and then dashed away when called to help set the table.

Jess straightened and rubbed her chest. "Maybe I'll write a memoir someday."

Jay extended a hand to Reece. "We meet at last. The man who won Jess's heart and saved the day."

Reece shook his hand. "I'm just Jess's sidekick during her battle with big pharma. She saved the day. Saved lives."

She felt a slight lump in her throat. He had explained to her that if she hadn't come back for him and stalled Shoup long enough for the Rider sniper to get in position, Reece would be dead.

"We're happy to finally meet you."

"I'll take your coats," her mom said. She took Jess's, hung it up, then took Reece's.

He offered to help, but she waved him off.

"Do you like dumplings?" she asked Reece as she situated his jacket on the hanger in the coat closet and smoothed down the length of it.

"I certainly do."

"Oh, what is this?" She pulled out a black velvet case from his jacket pocket and opened it.

"Mom!" Jess cried.

The room fell silent as all eyes stared at the diamond ring in her mother's hand.

Reece cleared his throat as he delicately reclaimed the box. He turned toward Jess. "I had anticipated asking you this evening after your family and I had a chance to become acquainted. I'd imagined the two of us on the back porch in the snow under a starlit sky."

How did he know her parents' house had a back porch? Of course he knew. Did he go anywhere—even to Christmas dinner—unprepared and not knowing every escape route?

"But under the mistletoe will do." He took her hand and led her two steps to the right.

Her brother grinned widely, and her mom clasped her hands over her mouth as Reece bent to one knee. Heat rose into Jess's cheeks.

"Reece?" Was this real? She knew he was the only man for her, but was he sure *he* was ready?

"Jess, you know better than anyone how flawed I am and the mistakes I've made, especially in taking my sweet time to commit to a relationship with you. I fell so hard and fast for you, it scared me. I ran away from you—more than once—when I should have been running toward you. It's taken almost losing you to acknowledge that I don't want to live without you. Will you build a life with me?" He raised the ring to her.

How had he gotten the perfect ring? Perfect cut? She considered how his best friend was married to her best friend, but even if Jenna hadn't told him, Claire probably could have found an internet trail going back five years to every piece of jewelry Jess had ever looked at. Reece had the resources to know exactly what type of ring she wanted. It was probably a perfect fit too. But she knew something he didn't—he could have proposed with a piece of string, and she would have accepted the offer.

"Yes, Reece. Yes."

He stood and slipped the ring onto her finger. "I love you."

"I love you."

They wrapped their arms around each other, and Jess closed her eyes to relish the feel of his strength and devotion. She could feel his heart racing against her chest and was somehow all the more swept off her feet by his nervousness.

With their lips pressed together under the mistletoe, she embraced their commitment to build a life together.

<<<THE END>>>

DEAR READER

If you enjoyed this book and want to know about future releases by CB Samet you can CLICK HERE to sign up for my mailing list! I promise I won't spam you. I only send an email when I have a new book released, giveaways, or special discounts. And I'll never sell your information. You can also unsubscribe at any time.

Also, as an independent author, I rely heavily on readers to spread the word about books they've read. If you enjoyed this story, kindly let others know by posting a brief comment on social media or leave a review where you purchased it.

Click below to follow me on Bookbub or Instagram!

Thank you for reading,
CB Samet
www.cbsamet.com

THE RIDER FILES SERIES

Meridian File, Book 1

Masters File, Book 2

McMillan File, Book 3

Maltisse File, Book 4

Storm File, Book 5

Sullivan File, Book 6

Sharp File, Book 7 (coming 2022)

ALSO BY CB SAMET

Romancing the Spirit Series

Clean Paranormal Romantic Suspense

"A collection of well-executed ... tales of love and ghosts."
—*Kirkus Reviews (on Romancing the Spirit Series, Novellas 1-6)*

Novella's 1-6 boxed set

Novella's 7-12 boxed set

Sadie's Sprit

Willow's Windfall

Cassie's Chase

Phoebe's Pharaoh

Vanessa's Valentine

Autumn's Angel

Carol's Christmas

Allison's Alibi

Gracelynn's Genie

Michelle's Miracle

Heather's Hero

Chloe's Cupid

Sabrina's Storm

Jenny's Justice

Stella's Star

Gigi's Gift

Phoenix's Phantom

The Dr. Whyte Thriller Series:

Black Gold

Whyte Knight

Gray Horizon

SAMPLE CHAPTER: JENNY'S JUSTICE

When prosecuting attorney Jenny Wiley sees the ghost of a murder victim, her hunt for justice thrusts her into a world of secrets and danger. Can Jenny stop the killer, or will she be the next victim?

A fast-paced, clean enemies-to-lovers romantic suspense thriller with a paranormal twist.

"Why do you want to ruin a good thing?" he demanded.

A wave of rage surged inside him. How dare Cecilia try to blackmail him? Did she comprehend who he was?

He'd tried to reason with her, but the conversation had escalated to arguing, followed by threatening. They'd had a mutually beneficial relationship. He'd paid for her time and expertise. Now she was pulling this stunt?

They argued in her living room—a minuscule space with a

small television and a couch that smelled like a perfume shop. He struggled to keep his voice low. No one could know he was there. He wouldn't have even come to this dump if she hadn't turned against him.

"Everybody gets mad. But everybody pays," the woman's pupils were pinpoint—tiny little beads in a sea of blue fire.

No wonder she was being so brazen. She was high on drugs. She'd told him her routine once: amphetamines in the morning, cocaine in the afternoon, sedatives when she needed to sleep.

She knew how to regulate the drugs she gave herself, and nights with her intoxicated made for a fun time. But this drug addict thought she was going to get away with blackmailing him? Not in his lifetime.

"Drop it," he snapped, the force of his words driving her backward and into the kitchen—another tiny room with bland white cabinets and cheap laminate countertops.

"I'm not paying you a penny. You think you'll ruin me? I'll ruin you," he said.

"What are you going to do?" Cecilia scoffed. "Send me to jail for drug charges? Been there, done that. I'll be out in a less than a month. I don't have anything to lose. You, on the other hand, have a career, a house—well, a couple of them—and probably wife number three in the pipeline. You have a lot to lose, so don't try to go head-to-head with me." She poked a long acrylic nail into his chest with each of the last several words.

He panicked as fury filled every crevice of his mind. He did have a great deal to lose. He couldn't let her get away with this. On primal instinct, before he understood his own actions, his hand closed over the handle of one of her kitchen knives.

And then there was blood. So much blood.

Jenny sat at the prosecutor's table watching the jury follow the defense attorney's every move.

He walked gracefully in his shimmering slate suit and spoke in a deep, authoritative voice like liquid satin as he began his opening statement. Like a fine, expensive bourbon—a burn so smooth you actually enjoyed it. "My name is Beaufort Montrose, but people call me Beau. Now, South Carolinians pronounce Beaufort as Bew-furt. Here in North Carolina, we say Bo-fert. To keep it simple, call me Beau."

Jenny suppressed an eye-roll. If she had a golden coin for every time she had to hear Beau Montrose talk about his name, she'd have a collection to rival her father's. And yet, the jury always melted into an adoring puddle at Beau's feet. Some combination of his impeccable hair, captivating blue eyes, confident stroll, and melodic voice lured them to his side. Of course, as the prosecuting attorney, she was immune to his charm.

SONG OF THE SIREN.

She scratched the words into her notebook with her black ballpoint pen. The smell from the ink wafted toward her.

What did she have to combat Beau's glamor? Her suit was from a mall department store and never seemed to look crisp despite her ironing. Her thick blonde hair was pulled back in a bun— because who had time for anything else? At least her bangs were even. Mostly. Her name certainly didn't have a movie star vibe like Beaufort Montrose.

The adoring jury watched Beau's every move as they sat in black high-back chairs behind a half wall of polished mahogany. Behind Jenny, the wooden pews were packed with spectators.

"Now, Miss Jenny Wiley here will try to convince you my client has broken the law," Beau continued eloquently. "But I ask you to carefully focus on the facts—and the facts only. Be careful not to confuse established facts with loose conjecture."

Truth, Jenny reminded herself. She had truth on her side. She reached into her pocket and rubbed the coin she carried as she glanced at the defendant.

Guilty.

She had the truth: the defendant had pulled the trigger and killed his employer. When Jenny walked the jury through events as they'd unfolded leading up to the murder, the jury would see the truth. No high-priced defense attorney—not even the best in Charlotte—could hide Bubba Hollins' guilt.

Work your magic, Beau. It's all smoke and mirrors.

⸻

Beau Montrose caught sight of the assistant district attorney leaving one of the judges' chambers.

He quickened his pace to catch up to her. "Fraternizing with the judge," he teased.

Jenny Wiley shot him a look of daggers without slowing her pace. Her heels clicked on the marble flooring. Beau chuckled. She was fun to rile, and her reputation was so squeaky clean they both knew his words were weightless.

"Nice presentation this morning," he continued. "Although you wasted too much breath on a case I'll win."

"Not this time," she said.

He arched an eyebrow. "Such confidence."

Her tone of conviction was one of her tells—like a gambler; whenever Jenny insisted the defendant was undeniably guilty, Beau's job became an interesting, uphill battle. He felt a little giddy at the thought he'd be in for a challenge.

Jenny Wiley brought his acquittal ratings down—though he was still one of the most sought-after defense attorneys in the city. The damage to his record was mildly irksome but perhaps a needed dose of humility. She posed a challenge—an exciting call to action to be on the top of his game. And because she was a formidable adversary, the victory against her would be that much sweeter.

He glanced at her apparel. Her charcoal suit fit her slender figure nicely and revealed shapely calves. A faint ginger-orange fragrance wafted off of her.

"There are a throng of reporters out there," he mentioned mildly—a warning so she wouldn't be caught off guard.

She hesitated and touched her hair. The bun she'd started the day with had developed rogue fly-away strands, but they only added to her beauty.

"Miss Wiley, I wasn't suggesting you look unprepared. On the contrary, you look quite lovely," Beau said.

She frowned. "I don't like reporters."

"Allow me. I'm happy to address them first. See if I can calm them down before you address them."

She eyed him suspiciously as if wondering if he was playing her.

He wasn't manipulating her, but she was free to think what she liked. His job description was to impress clients with his bold brand and media show, not impress anyone in the DA's office. Some prosecutors disdained his flare but others understood the purpose of his theatrics. Sadly, Jenny had always unmistakably fallen in the disdain category.

"After you." She gestured.

He gave a polite nod before stepping outside. His smile widened. "If it pleases the press," he said to the crowd of reporters, "I can take just a few questions." He made a show of checking his watch.

All eyes focused on him. The volley of anticipated questions came at him.

"Do you have any evidence to refute the State's case?"

"How will you handle the witnesses who say they saw your client leaving the scene of the crime?"

After grabbing a latte, Jenny returned to her office to work on additional legal notes. She felt like she'd made a solid case against Bubba, but logic and truth didn't always prevail in the courtroom, especially when Beau Montrose was on the opposing team.

She acknowledged that her discontent with him stemmed from simultaneously admiring what an outstanding lawyer he was and disliking his peacock-display of strutting around the courtroom. His media antics added to her irritation, but that behavior was exactly what his clients wanted.

Her office was small, but she was one of eighty-five assistant district attorneys, so office space was always a negotiation and source of contention.

"Jenny," a voice greeted her at her door.

She looked up from her paperwork to see Stu Winslow, Charlotte's shinning District Attorney, standing in her doorway. Stu wore a gray suit over a white shirt and red tie. His black leather shoes had been polished to shine.

Despite his perfectly waved blond hair turning white, neighborly charm, and easy smile, his presence set Jenny on edge. Stu didn't appear in the doorway of an underling's office unless he wanted something.

"How are you, Stu?" She'd learned the hard way not to ask what she could do for him or why he was there when he spontaneously arrived at her doorway. If he wanted something from her, she wouldn't make it so easy.

"I'm doing well. I wanted to see how you're fairing after your opening remarks on such a high-profile case."

He'd been hovering incessantly ever since she'd been assigned lead on the Bubba Hollins case. She supposed the trial of the son of a congressman who'd supported Stu's election made him nervous. Since she wasn't an elected official, she didn't have a problem throwing her full capabilities into the case to convict a murderer. Stu had voiced his concerns about her being junior, even though she was part of the Homicide Team of prosecutors. She'd argued her track-record indicated she was ready.

When he hadn't backed her a hundred percent, Jenny had refrained from reminding Stu of the many other cases she'd helped him prepare. When his success had been in some part due to her efforts, she'd been given no credit for her impact.

But that was okay; she was biding her time. All of the effort was part of office politics. She scratched his back; he'd scratch hers. When the time came for promotion or larger cases, more prominent cases, Stu would remember how she'd been a team player. He would remember, wouldn't he?

Reaching into her jacket pocket, she rubbed the coin, feeling the textured surface. "I've got wisdom, justice, courage, and temperance on my side. I'll be just fine." She had evidence also, but that didn't guarantee a win.

"That's good, because I watched Beau Montrose putting on a display at the press conference, and I didn't see you countering—reassuring the community that the killer would remain behind bars."

"I assure you, the killer will remain behind bars. I gave my statement after Beau. The media chose not to air it."

Stu smiled, somehow wide but not friendly. "Okay. Okay. These career-making cases are tricky things. They can also be career-ending."

Beau watched Jenny's closing arguments with interest. She'd prepared a precise summation, emphasizing key points in the trial without regurgitating all of the details to a saturated jury. She appealed to their analytical reasoning and not their emotion. Without straying from the facts, she kept her arguments concise.

Beau had represented his client as best he could—letting the burden of proof fall on the prosecutor. He'd raised credibility issues with witnesses, where applicable, and argued against small time-table discrepancies which existed.

But the prosecution had a solid case, and Bubba Hollins had been unwilling to plead guilty.

Jenny spoke with a soft voice, yet still commanded the room. She and Beau had been on opposing teams for several years now as he built up his practice in Charlotte, but he knew very little about her personally outside of work.

That probably wasn't going to change. Jenny was a straight arrow, no nonsense, no fraternizing with the enemy sort of person. And Beau preferred not to entangle himself in the type of drama that would befall him should he pursue the whimsical idea of getting to know Jenny Wiley.

When the session was adjourned to let the jury deliberate, Beau stepped into the hallway and checked his phone.

Five missed calls and three text messages.

He debated for a moment whether to respond to these now or take a few minutes to see if his client needed reassurance. Bubba had been mostly rude, arrogant, demanding, and demeaning throughout the course of this trial. Beau had enough self-worth that Bubba's behavior didn't bother him. He also understood that his clients were under a great amount of stress and their behavior wasn't always reflective of their true personality. However, he didn't think this statement applied to Bubba Hollins.

With that in mind, Beau opted not to play the role of consolatory hand-holder but listened to his voicemail instead.

He stepped over to one corner by the window to avoid the crowd awaiting the jury's verdict.

"Beau, this is Karl." His cousin's voice sounded edgy and distraught. "This is my one phone call, man. I need your help. I'm in jail. Cecilia is dead, and they think I murdered her."

<<CONTINUE READING ON ALL MAJOR RETAILERS>>